to having FU...

April

Challenge your mates to an egg painting competition. Use paints to decorate your cold, hard-boiled eggs in any way you like, then ask someone to judge which is the best. A **chocolate** egg would be an ideal prize, cos you could all share it (maybe!!).

May

Start by washing your face in the early morning dew on May 1st. If you do, it's said that you will look beautiful all year. Then invite some friends to join you for a picnic. If the weather's nice you can all sit in the garden or, if it's wet, decorate your room with bunches of artificial flowers to make it **look** like a garden.

June

Organise a cricket match. If you have a week or two to spare, ask Dad to explain the rules - alternatively, you can improvise and make your **own** rules. This is better done in advance though, as making the rules up as you go along can cause lots of arguments. Have **fun**!

£6.99

what's in...?

2. **Fun!** Things to do, places to go
5. **Happy Families** Your first fabby photo story
10. **Byker Beauties!** Behind the scenes at Byker Grove
13. **The Comp** Tune in to Radio Redvale
20. **Spring** Wordsearch
21. **Girl Zone** Be prepared
22. **How Good A Friend Are You?** Find out here
24. **Wild** Poster
25. **Annie!** Will there be a happy ending?
30. **All Made Up!** How to say sorry
32. **Exchange!** A mystery for Mia
34. **Summer** Wordsearch
35. **The Four Marys** Your favourite foursome
43. **Hide 'n' Seek!** Try our mega maze
44. **Weather Watch** Look to the skies – and more
46. **Purr-fect Pet!** Cat-speak made simple
48. **Friends For Ever?** Hours of fun for all
50. **Wild** Poster
51. **Just Like Jolie** Cool photo story
57. **Top To Toe** Fun fashion flowchart
58. **It Happened To Me...** A reader's story
59. **Matchmaker!** Cate's on a mission
65. **Snapped!** Picture puzzles
66. **Star Force!** Are you a Goody or a Baddy?
70. **Autumn** Wordsearch
71. **Wild** Poster
72. **Toots** Bunty's model miss
74. **Acting Up!** Stage school secrets
76. **Animal Antics!** It's totally crazy
78. **Write On!** Meet author 'Zizou Corder'
80. **The Werewolf** Spooky story
82. **Feel The Heat!** Cool flowchart
83. **Wild** Poster
84. **Living Legends!** It's quiz time
86. **Girl Zone** Feed the birds
87. **The Secret!** Trouble when Sarah comes to stay
95. **Star Spot!** Pop poster
96. **Did You Know...?** Celebrity facts
98. **Celeb Cred Check!** How much do you know?
99. **The Comp** It's Christmas
105. **Wild** Poster
106. **Merry Christmas!** Festive game
108. **Word Power!** Puzzles – plain but not so simple
110. **Barking Mad!** It's dog-speak
112. **Puzzle Answers** They're all here
113. **The Four Marys** More fun at St Elmo's
119. **Wild** Poster
120. **Winter** Wordsearch
121. **Happy Birthday!** Your final fabby photostory
126. **Fun! July to December** More groovy things to do

Some material may have been previously published.

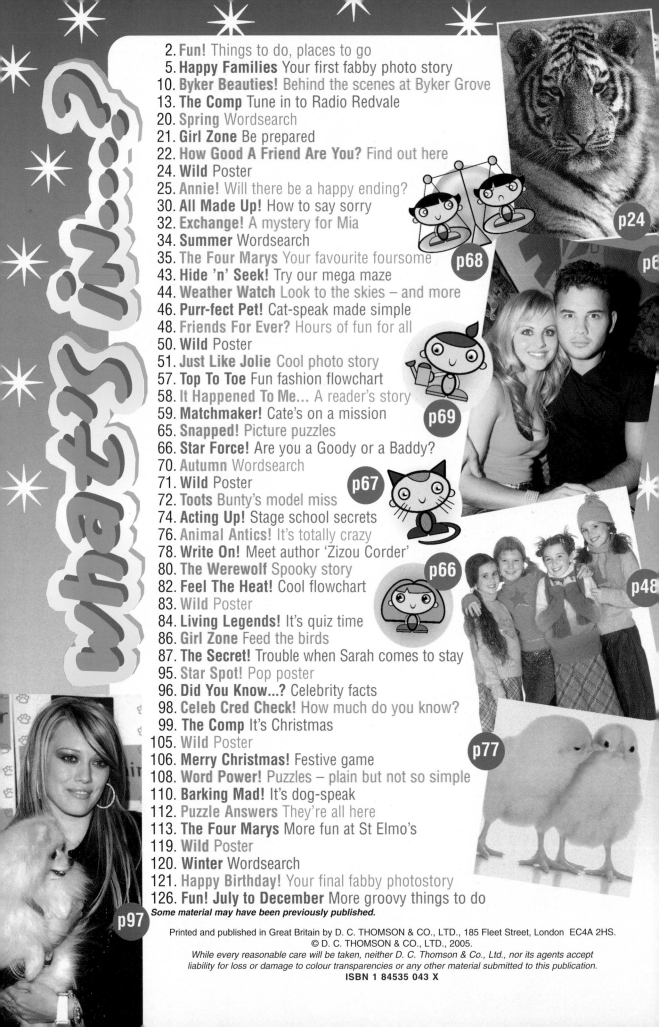

p24

p68

p69

p67

p66

p48

p77

p97

Printed and published in Great Britain by D. C. THOMSON & CO., LTD., 185 Fleet Street, London EC4A 2HS.
© D. C. THOMSON & CO., LTD., 2005.
*While every reasonable care will be taken, neither D. C. Thomson & Co., Ltd., nor its agents accept
liability for loss or damage to colour transparencies or any other material submitted to this publication.*
ISBN 1 84535 043 X

Happy Families

5

IF HE'S GOING THROUGH A MESSY FAMILY SPLIT, HE'S NOT LIKELY TO WANT TO HAVE ANYTHING TO DO WITH ME — MISS HAPPY FAMILIES!

But, later —

HI. SAM ISN'T IT? IF YOU'RE GOING TO FRENCH, I'LL — ER — I'LL WALK ALONG WITH YOU.

NO. I — I HAVE TO CALL AT THE OFFICE FIRST. YOU GO ON AHEAD.

I HATE TO BE OFF WITH HIM, BUT I COULD NEVER INTRODUCE HIM TO MY 'PERFECT' FAMILY. IT WOULD BE TOO CRUEL.

Sam managed to avoid Dean. Then, on the last day of term —

I'M DREADING THE HOLS. MUM AND DAD ARE ALREADY ARGUING ABOUT HOW LONG I'VE TO STAY WITH EACH OF THEM.

POOR YOU, LUCY.

AND POOR ME, TOO. LOOK LIKE DEAN'S FOUND A GIRL WHO IS INTERESTED.

STILL, I COULDN'T EXPECT HIM TO STAY INTERESTED IN ME WHEN I WAS SO OFF WITH HIM. I JUST WISH I DIDN'T FANCY HIM SO MUCH.

A few days later —

HOW ABOUT WE GO TO ROSEWALK PARK AT THE WEEKEND? YOU CAN EACH BRING A MATE.

GREAT, DAD. I'LL ASK TOBY.

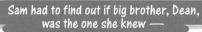

8

9

Byker Beauties!

Ever wondered how the characters you see on TV achieve their 'look'? We spoke to some of the girls from Byker Grove, and asked them to share a few 'behind the camera' secrets!

Moisturised .

Hannah and Chelsea are relative newcomers to the cast, so it's all still quite exciting for them.

Concealed . . .

H ANNAH, who plays ZOE, is first in the dentist's — sorry, make-up artist's — chair. Hannah's face is made up with a moisturiser, followed by a foundation to even out skin tones, and then blusher to give her skin a natural look.

A very fine brown eyeliner is used to accentuate her eyes and a little under-eye concealer is applied. This concealer is very important, as it is light reflective and makes sure Hannah doesn't look as if she has dark shadows under her eyes when she appears on screen.

Hannah's hair is then straightened and an extra-strong hair spray is used to hold her hair in place. As Zoe's look doesn't change much, Hannah has her hair trimmed every four weeks so that it always looks the same on screen.

Styled . .

Next up is CHELSEA who plays LUCY. Chelsea is looking smug because she has lovely skin and, as a result, doesn't need much make-up — even for TV. For a scene where Lucy had a date she wore mascara and lip-gloss. But, generally, she only has a little concealer put under her eyes. However, as Lucy's hair is a feature of her character, they try to do something different with it for every show — and that can take ages.

Brushed . . .

Straightened . . .

Tugged . . .

Like models, the girls are told to arrive on set with clean, natural hair, so the stylists can start work right away.
Chelsea's hair is first brushed, then straightened and calmed with a hair serum. It is then twisted and styled into any one of a variety of styles. Side ponytail, bun, spiky twist — Lucy has had them all and more.

Then twisted into shape.

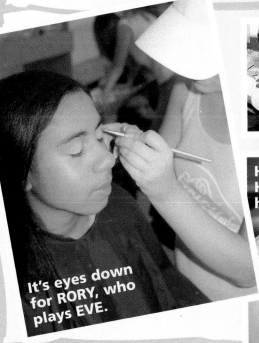

It's eyes down for RORY, who plays EVE.

For more experienced members of the cast, the make-up can take a bit longer — but then again, the girls can always help out by doing some of it themselves.

Now turn over to see the finished looks.

HEATHER, who plays HAYLEY, lends a helping hand.

Hannah loves the look that is created for her — and she loves having her make-up done, too. In fact, she likes it so much that she'd like to be a make-up artist when she's older. She hates having to get up early to go on shoots, though. "I sometimes leave it too late to eat," she says. "But we have breakfast made for us when we get here, so it isn't too bad."

Chelsea

Hannah

Chelsea loves her Lucy look and considers herself very lucky because she landed the part by answering an ad in the paper. "There were about 60 or 70 girls to begin with," she told us, "so I was thrilled to be chosen." Chelsea loves singing and dancing and if she doesn't do that as a career, she'd like to be a director — cos she likes being in charge.

Rory is the only cast member who doesn't come from the north east of England, so when she is filming she stays in a hotel with her mum. "I love everything about being in Byker Grove," she said. "I've been acting since I was quite young, though, so I hope to make it my career."

Heather

Rory

Heather would like to go on playing Hayley in Byker Grove for ever, but once the cast members reach 17, they have to leave. "I'd like to be like Ant and Dec and go on to make different TV programmes," she said. "But I know I'll still have to stick in at school, too."

I FANCY DOING SOMETHING ABOUT LOS ANGELES, AND HOW DIFFERENT LIFE IS THERE. MY SISTER, CARLY, LIVES THERE, SO SHE'LL HELP ME I'M SURE.

SOUNDS COOL, ROZ.

BO-RING! *I'M* GOING TO DO A CHART AND FASHION SHOW.

D'UH! HARDLY ORIGINAL, JAYNE.

AH, BUT I'LL GIVE IT MY OWN SLANT. BESIDES, WHO WANTS TO LISTEN TO A BORING OLD SCHOOL HISTORY?

I HATE TO AGREE WITH JAYNE THE PAIN, BUT I THINK SHE'S GOT A POINT ABOUT BECKY AND HAYLEY'S IDEA.

TROY, GARY, HODGE AND I THOUGHT WE'D DO A PROGRAMMED ABOUT FOOTBALL. AFTER ALL, WE'RE EXPERTS.

AT LOSING, ANYWAY, FREDDY. BUT SERIOUSLY, I THINK THAT'S A GREAT IDEA. CAN I HELP?

NO WAY, BRADY. WHAT DO GIRLS KNOW ABOUT FOOTBALL?

MORE THAN *YOU*, ANYWAY, TROY GILLAN.

OH, YEAH? LIKE HOW BECKHAM'S STYLED HIS HAIR THIS WEEK, NO DOUBT. FORGET IT, GIRLIE.

I HEARD THAT, LAURA. PIGS! BUT CHEER UP. YOU CAN HELP HAYLEY AND ME.

THANKS, BECKY.

AT LEAST I'LL BE DOING *SOMETHING*.

14

So, that weekend —

WOW, BECKS! LOOK AT THIS. THERE WAS AN EARLIER SCHOOL BUILT ON THE SITE. IT WAS PULLED DOWN TO MAKE WAY FOR THE COMP.

GLADSTONE ROAD MODERN SCHOOL. IT SOUNDS REALLY WEIRD.

LOCAL HISTORY

MAYBE WE SHOULD TRY AND FIND SOMEONE WHO WENT THERE?

THE TWINS SOUND SO EXCITED ABOUT ALL THIS — BUT I'M BORED. I THINK I'LL MAKE AN EXCUSE AND LEAVE.

Later, the twins met Nikki and Claire —

. . . SO WE'D LOVE TO FIND AN OLD PUPIL.

I'LL ASK MY GREAT GRAN IF SHE REMEMBERS ANYTHING, BECKY. SHE'S LIVED AROUND HERE FOR ALL HER LIFE.

COOL, NIKKI. YOU AND CLAIRE CAN JOIN OUR TEAM IF YOU LIKE.

SMALL PROB, HAYLEY. I'M HEARING IMPAIRED, REMEMBER? YOU CAN'T LIP-READ A RADIO.

OOOOPS! I FORGOT, CLAIRE. BUT THERE'LL BE HEAPS OF STUFF YOU CAN DO TO HELP, ANYWAY.

Meanwhile —

HI, GUYS, HOW'S THE CUTTING EDGE SPORTS SHOW GOING?

IT ISN'T — NOT FOR ME AND HODGE, ANYWAY.

GARY AND TROY WANT TO DO EVERYTHING THEIR WAY. THEY DON'T EVEN LISTEN TO FREDDY AND ME.

IT'S LIKE, 'HI, I'M GARY, AND I'M GOING TO TALK ABOUT MY FAVOURITE FOOTBALL TEAM AND MY FAVOURITE PLAYERS.'

HA, HA, HA! THAT'S DEAD GOOD, HODGE. HE SHOULD REMEMBER HE'S GARY LISTER — NOT GARY LINEKER.

YEAH! AND TROY THINKS HE'S ALAN HANSEN! PITY WE CAN'T DO SOMETHING TO BRING THEM DOWN A PEG OR TWO.

HEY! WHY DON'T WE DO A COMEDY SHOW WITH SKETCHES ABOUT SCHOOL, AND IDIOTS LIKE GARY AND TROY?

GREAT IDEA. HODGE CAN DO ALL SORTS OF FUNNY VOICES, YOU KNOW.

AND I'VE GOT A SOUND EFFECTS CD.

THAT'S SETTLED. LET'S START JOTTING DOWN OUR IDEAS RIGHT NOW!

Things weren't going so well for Roz.

I'M GETTING NOWHERE FAST. STANCEE'S TRYING TO HELP — BUT ALL HER INFORMATION COMES FROM AMERICAN TV SHOWS. I WISH CARLY WOULD HURRY UP AND RING ME BACK. I WANT IDEAS FROM SOMEONE WHO'S ACTUALLY *LIVING* IN THE STATES.

Then —

HI, ROZ. KIKO HERE. I HEARD ABOUT YOUR IDEA FOR THE RADIO PROGRAMME AND WONDERED IF YOU'D LET AMY AND ME HELP. MY COUSIN'S JUST MOVED TO CALIFORNIA AND SHE'S GIVEN ME SOME GREAT IDEAS.

REALLY, KIKO? BRILLIANT! I'LL SEE YOU AND AMY ON MONDAY AND WE CAN TALK ABOUT IT.

And —

I PHONED MY COUSIN AND TAPED LOTS OF INFO. SHE'S GOING TO E-MAIL ME MORE ABOUT THE DIFFERENCES BETWEEN HER NEW HOME AND TOKYO.

THAT'S EXCELLENT. WE CAN COMPARE SCHOOL LIFE IN JAPAN AS WELL AS IN THE STATES.

Soon all the projects were underway —

MY GREAT GRAN RANG MRS HERBERT YESTERDAY. SHE'S MADE A LIST ALREADY OF WHAT LIFE WAS LIKE AT GLADSTONE ROAD.

GREAT. I'VE BROUGHT ALONG DAD'S DICTAPHONE, TOO, JUST IN CASE WE FORGET ANYTHING.

16

YOU'LL HAVE TO SPEAK CLEARLY, LUVVIES. I'M DEAF AND USUALLY LIP READ OR SIGN.

NO PROBS. YOU ASK THE QUESTIONS, BECKY, AND I'LL SIGN.

So —

WHAT WAS THE FOOD LIKE, MRS HERBERT?

I REMEMBER WE HAD CABBAGE AND TAPIOCA PUDDING A LOT. I'VE NEVER LIKED EITHER SINCE!

Eventually —

THAT WAS BRILLIANT, NIKKI. AND WELL DONE, CLAIRE. WE'VE LOADS OF STUFF FOR THE FIRST PART OF THE SHOW.

WE CAN START ON THE EARLY YEARS OF OUR OWN SCHOOL NEXT.

The sketch show was coming on, too —

'AND NOW IT'S OVER TO OUR SPORTS REPORTER, WILLIE WINNIT, FOR THE LATEST ON THE EGG AND SPOON PENALTY SHOOT OUT!'

HONESTLY! HOW CHILDISH!

SO HOW'S YOUR PROGRAMME GOING, JAYNE?

GREAT. I'VE MANAGED TO GET AN INTERVIEW WITH A FASHION DESIGNER. I TELL YOU, MY SPOT ON REDVALE FM IS A DONE DEAL.

Gary and Troy were just as confident —

THEY'LL BE NO ONE TO TOUCH US.

REDVALE FM HERE WE COME.

At last the day arrived to record the demos —

WE'VE SET UP A SMALL SOUND STUDIO NEXT DOOR. THE SOUND ENGINEER, WILF, WILL HELP YOU RECORD AND EDIT YOUR MINI DISCS DOWN TO TEN MINUTES.

Jayne went first —

I WISH I COULD BE *HALF* AS CONFIDENT AS HER. HOW DO YOU FEEL, LAURA?

SICK! BUT AT LEAST I'VE . . . OH, LOOK WHO'S HERE. *CARLY!*

HI, GIRLS. WE'VE GOT OUR OWN REAL-LIFE L.A. GAL TO GIVE THE LOW-DOWN ON LIFE IN THE SMOG. BETTER THAN A PHONE CALL, EH?

COOL, ROZ. AND HI, CARLY. DON'T THINK I WAS EVER AS PLEASED TO SEE *ANYONE!*

WISH I COULD SAY THE SAME. I'M STILL TERRIFIED!

ME TOO. EVERYONE ELSE SEEMS TO HAVE MORE INTERESTING PROGRAMMES THAN US.

I'M SURE TO FORGET MY WORDS.

But, eventually —

THAT'S IT, FOLKS. YOUR DEMO TAPES WILL BE JUDGED BY MR BURNS, AND THE WINNERS WILL BE ANNOUNCED ON FRIDAY.

WELL DONE, ALL. SOME OF YOU SHOW REAL TALENT!

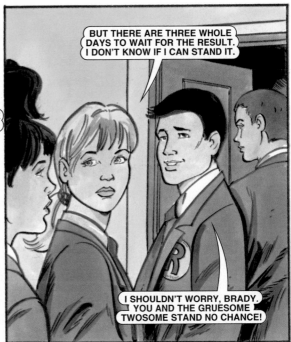

the end

Spring

Find these words hidden up, down, backwards, forwards and diagonally in our special spring wordsearch. Letters can be used more than once and the unused letters will spell out some things we *love* about spring.

T	R	E	S	✿	L	E	S	I	N	B	T
L	O	D	D	D	A	S	D	R	A	C	S
S	U	S	R	U	M	✿	A	S	G	G	E
B	O	A	I	C	B	M	F	R	C	A	N
E	U	L	B	K	S	R	F	E	R	S	N
Y	D	L	H	L	A	O	O	W	O	H	C
E	S	E	T	I	C	R	D	O	C	O	H
L	D	R	N	N	O	G	I	L	U	W	I
L	U	B	✿	G	R	S	L	F	S	E	C
O	O	M	R	E	T	S	A	E	✿	R	K
W	L	U	E	P	U	D	D	L	E	S	S
S	C	N	B	U	P	I	L	U	T	N	S

birds
blue
buds
cards
chicks
clouds
crocus
daffodil
duckling
easter
eggs
flowers
green
lambs
nest
puddles
rainbow
showers
tulip
umbrella
yellow

Hidden message:
Trees in blossom and hot cross buns!

20

Girl Zone

HI, BUNTY. COMING DOWN TO THE PARK WITH ME 'N' LISA?

EH? YOU MUST BE JOKIN', JO. IT'S RAINING!

TCH! DON'T BE A PAIN. IT'S ONLY DRIZZLE!

YEAH! A LITTLE RAIN WON'T HURT YOU.

WELL — I SUPPOSE IT'LL BE OKAY.

BUT I'LL TAKE MY UMBRELLA.

I DON'T BELIEVE IT, LISA. I THINK SHE'S AFRAID SHE'LL MELT.

HA, HA, HA!

LAUGH IF YOU LIKE. BUT I'LL HAVE THE LAST LAUGH WHEN YOU'RE SOAKED AND I'M BONE DRY.

And —

YOUR 'DRIZZLE'S' A BIT HEAVIER NOW, ISN'T IT? BET YOU WISH YOU HAD A BROLLY LIKE ME.

HERE YOU ARE, DUCKS. SOME NICE TASTY CRUMBS.

COME ON, B. LET'S GET HOME BEFORE . . .

AAAGH! I'M SLIPPING!

SPLASH

ER — I DON'T SUPPOSE YOU'LL NEED YOUR UMBRELLA NOW, BUNTY.

HUH! VERY FUNNY!

TYPICAL! I BRING THE BROLLY — BUT I STILL END UP BEING THE ONE WHO'S REALLY SOAKED!

21

How Good A Friend

1

Your best friend tries out a weird new hairstyle. Do you...
a) Giggle every time you look at her?
b) Suggest another style which might be better?
c) Say you like it?

2

A friend forgets to send you a holiday postcard. How do you react?
a) Say she must have been having a great time.
b) Laugh. After all, you forgot her birthday last year.
c) Go in a mega huff and refuse to speak to her.

3

You discover that your friend is being bullied. What do you do?
a) Nothing. She's the only one who can make things better.
b) Keep out of it in case you get bullied as well.
c) Tell her to get help from a teacher or her parents.

22

Are You?

4 **Your best friend doesn't like your new boyfriend. Do you...**
a) Chuck him – no boy is worth losing your pal?
b) Arrange to meet them at different times?
c) Tell her she'll grow to like him in time?

5

A friend has just been chucked by her first boyfriend. What would you do?
a) Say you're glad. You never liked him, anyway.
b) Provide a box of tissues – and a shoulder to cry on.
c) Text her and say you'll be in touch later.

6

A new girl starts tagging on to you and your friend. How do you feel?
a) Annoyed cos three's a crowd.
b) Scared in case she's trying to steal your friend.
c) Pleased. The more the merrier.

7 **Your mate's late for the cinema. Do you...**
a) Call her to find out what the problem is?
b) Storm round and demand an explanation?
c) Go home all upset?

8 **Your pal wants you to play tennis three times a week. What do you do?**
a) Say you will, then think up lots of excuses.
b) Agree to go once a week. You've other things to do, too.
c) Say okay and hope she goes off the idea very soon.

Now add up your scores

1. a) 1   b) 2   c) 3
2. a) 2   b) 1   c) 3
3. a) 1   b) 3   c) 2
4. a) 2   b) 3   c) 1
5. a) 3   b) 2   c) 1
6. a) 1   b) 3   c) 2
7. a) 2   b) 1   c) 3
8. a) 1   b) 2   c) 3

13 – 20
You're at your best when you're with your mates, because you just love being a friend. You're thoughtful and considerate – but with a mind of your own, too. You're always prepared to listen and laugh — and you can give good advice when it's needed. Well done you!

8 – 12
You love your friends, that's for sure, but you love yourself even more. No one expects you to do exactly what your friends want all the time, but try not to be selfish and remember that other people have feelings, too. Try putting your friends first now and again.

21 – 27
You want to be a good friend so much that you often forget to be yourself. You don't always have to agree with what others say or go along with what they want, you know. Try standing up for yourself a bit more and you'll probably find that people like you even better.

Annie!

IT was April 1885 and ten-year-old Annie Freeman and her parents had just moved to the tiny village of Brockridge —

MORNING, LASS! LOOKS LIKE IT'LL BE A GRAND DAY.

I'VE JUST THE HENS TO FEED, MUM, AND THEN I'LL GET READY FOR SCHOOL.

YOU'RE A GOOD GIRL, ANNIE! BUT DON'T BE LATE — I KNOW HOW MUCH YOU LOVE YOUR LESSONS.

GOOD MORNING, MISTER JACK! IT'S LOVELY, ISN'T IT? THE SPRING FLOWERS WILL SOON BE THROUGH.

ANNIE'S A GRAND LASS — ALWAYS READY WITH A SMILE AND A CHEERY WORD. YOU'D THINK SHE'D LIVED HERE ALL HER LIFE. WHAT BROUGHT HER FAMILY TO BROCKRIDGE?

NO ONE KNOWS. BUT IT DOES YOU GOOD TO SEE A LASS SO FULL OF LIFE AND LAUGHTER.

THERE'S THE SCHOOL BELL RINGING! I MUST HURRY. OH! POOR LITTLE DANNY'S FALLEN DOWN.

25

In class —

THAT'S A NASTY GRAZE, DANNY, BUT YOU'RE BEING VERY BRAVE. LOOK — YOU CAN TAKE THIS APPLE AS A REWARD.

OH, THANK YOU, ANNIE! I LOVE APPLES, BUT MY FAMILY IS TOO POOR TO AFFORD FRESH FRUIT.

MOVE OVER, SAM! I WANT TO SIT BESIDE ANNIE!

NO! I'M STAYING HERE. YOU SAT WITH HER YESTERDAY.

HUH! LOOK AT THOSE STUPID BRATS, ELLEN! FANCY WANTING TO SIT BESIDE MISS GOODY-GOODY!

Later —

WELL DONE, ANNIE! YOU CAN CLEAN THE BLACKBOARD NOW AND THEN HELP THE LITTLE ONES WITH THEIR WORK.

OH!

CAREFUL, ANNIE! YOU MIGHT HURT YOURSELF!

HA, HA, HA! SERVES HER RIGHT!

I'M SURE THAT WASN'T AN ACCIDENT. I'D LIKE TO BE FRIENDS WITH MARY AND ELLEN, BUT THEY DON'T LIKE ME. MAYBE IT'S BECAUSE I'M NEW HERE?

Later —

IT WILL SOON BE MAY DAY. TOMORROW WE MUST CHOOSE OUR MAY QUEEN AND PRACTISE THE MAYPOLE DANCE.

A MAY QUEEN! THERE WAS NEVER ANYTHING LIKE THIS IN TOWN. IT SOUNDS WONDERFUL!

On the way home —

THAT'S ONE OF FARMER GRAY'S HENS. SHE MUST HAVE A NEST IN THE HEDGE. I WONDER IF THERE ARE ANY EGGS?

27

All made

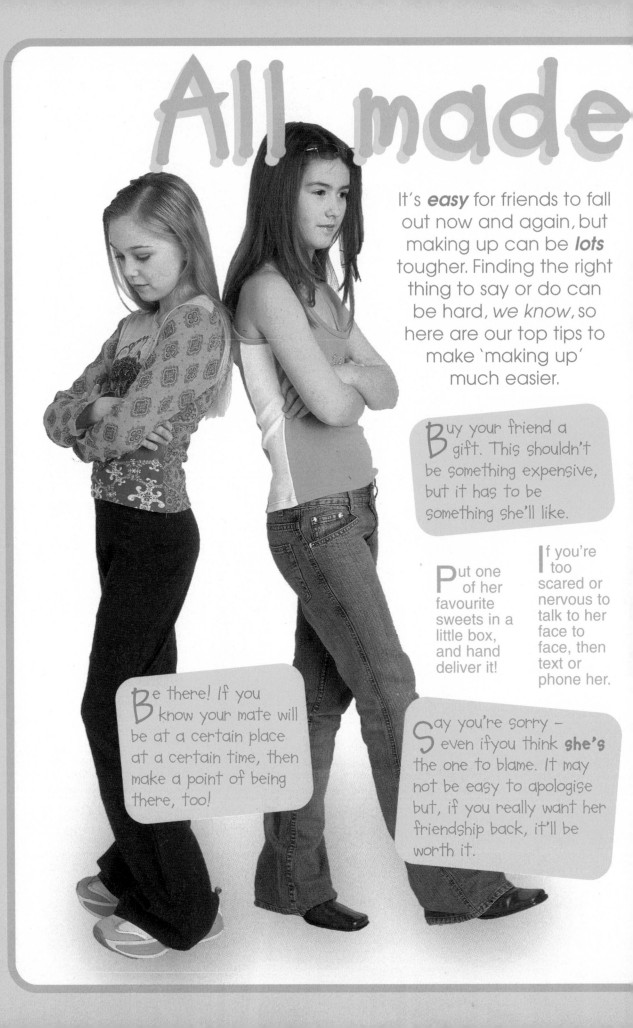

It's **easy** for friends to fall out now and again, but making up can be **lots** tougher. Finding the right thing to say or do can be hard, *we know*, so here are our top tips to make 'making up' much easier.

Buy your friend a gift. This shouldn't be something expensive, but it has to be something she'll like.

Put one of her favourite sweets in a little box, and hand deliver it!

If you're too scared or nervous to talk to her face to face, then text or phone her.

Be there! If you know your mate will be at a certain place at a certain time, then make a point of being there, too!

Say you're sorry – even if you think **she's** the one to blame. It may not be easy to apologise but, if you really want her friendship back, it'll be worth it.

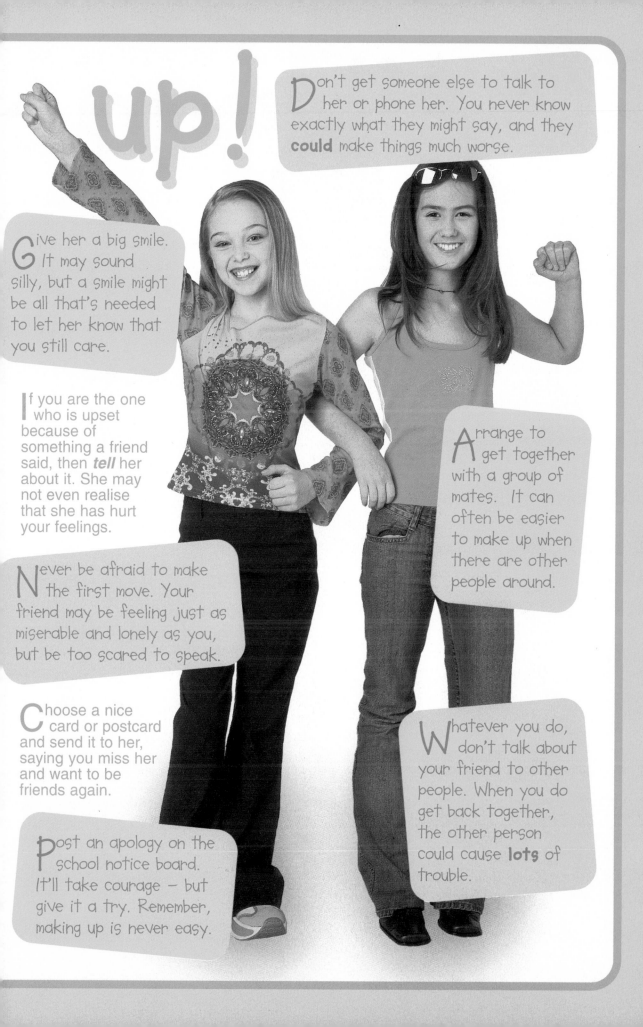

up!

Don't get someone else to talk to her or phone her. You never know exactly what they might say, and they **could** make things much worse.

Give her a big smile. It may sound silly, but a smile might be all that's needed to let her know that you still care.

If you are the one who is upset because of something a friend said, then **tell** her about it. She may not even realise that she has hurt your feelings.

Never be afraid to make the first move. Your friend may be feeling just as miserable and lonely as you, but be too scared to speak.

Arrange to get together with a group of mates. It can often be easier to make up when there are other people around.

Choose a nice card or postcard and send it to her, saying you miss her and want to be friends again.

Whatever you do, don't talk about your friend to other people. When you do get back together, the other person could cause **lots** of trouble.

Post an apology on the school notice board. It'll take courage — but give it a try. Remember, making up is never easy.

Exchange!

MINE seems a bit shy," said Gina. "Mine never stops complaining," said Bethany. "That's nothing," groaned Frances. "Mine took one look at me and said I was much fatter than in the class photo she was sent!"

The girls were discussing their French exchange visitors who had arrived the evening before. Mia's school had organised an exchange with another school in France, and it had been fun finding out which girl was allocated to which family.

So far, from what Mia could make

out, she hadn't done too badly. Her visitor, Corinne, was a quiet girl with straight black hair and a fringe. She smiled a lot, but seemed rather nervous. She didn't say very much, either, but that wasn't surprising because she had only been learning English for a year or so.

But there were a few things that seemed a little bit odd. For a start, she didn't seem to want to ring home at all. Mia's mum had Corinne's home number and, as soon as Corinne arrived, she called to say that the French girl had arrived safely. But Corinne didn't even want to speak to her mother.

"I will call later," she said before rushing to Mia's room, where she spent most of the evening sending text messages on her mobile phone.

"It's very odd," said Mia. "There's something that doesn't quite add up about her. I asked her how many sisters she had and she said three. Then, a couple of hours later, she said she only had one."

"That could be problems with her English," said Bethany.

"I know," agreed Mia, "but I'm sure she was tucking into a burger when we met her at the airport, yet when Mum read her info notes, they say she's vegetarian."

"Maybe it was a veggie burger," suggested Gina.

"Yeah! And maybe I'm the Queen of Sheba," said Mia. "There's definitely something odd."

At two o'clock the next morning, Mia woke with a start. There was something wrong — she just knew it. Then it dawned on her. She couldn't hear Corinne's gentle breathing from the other side of the room. She opened her eyes and glanced over towards the camp bed. It was empty — and there was no sign of Corrine anywhere in the room."

"Maybe she's gone to the bathroom," Mia thought. But there was no sign of her there, either — or downstairs.

Mia was just beginning to panic when she heard a noise from the attic and noticed that the loft ladder had been pulled down. What on earth was Corinne doing in the attic? There was only one way to find out.

As she reached the top, Mia's mouth dropped open. Standing near the window, talking on a mobile phone, was a girl about the same age and size as Corinne. She looked vaguely familiar but, instead of straight black hair, this girl had short blonde curls. Who on earth was she?

As the girl turned, Mia noticed something in her hand. It was a wig. A straight black bob with a heavy fringe. Corinne had been wearing a wig.

"So you see," said Mia triumphantly at school next day, "I told you there was something odd about her."

"But what on earth was she doing at two in the morning, in your attic, wearing a wig?" Frances was puzzled.

"She wasn't wearing a wig," Mia grinned. "She had taken her wig off. You see, the girl we thought was Corinne is really Aurelie. They're cousins, so they look alike — apart from the fact that Aurelie has blonde curly hair and Corinne is dark. Aurelie wanted to come to England, but her school was doing a German exchange — and Corinne fancied Germany rather than her school exchange here. So the two girls decide to do their very own exchange and swap places. They even swapped passports and, with wigs on, it was very difficult to tell them apart.

"The only problem was they sometimes forgot who they were — like when my exchange told me she had three sisters. The worst thing, though, was that the wigs began to itch. My visitor, Aurelie, couldn't stand it any longer, so that's why she was in our attic phoning Corinne at two o'clock in the morning."

"It seems incredible," said Bethany. "How come you have all the luck and get someone interesting? My exchange spent the whole of this morning moaning that she didn't like our breakfast cereal — or our milk."

"Oh, well," said Mia, with a twinkle in her eye, "I wouldn't complain too much, otherwise I might do an exchange with you. At least you've only got one visitor but, as of tomorrow, the real Corinne is coming to join her cousin, so I'm going to end up with two."

The End

Summer

The words below are all hidden in this hot summer wordsearch and can read forwards, backwards, up, down or diagonally. Once you have found all the words, the remaining letters will spell out something we look forward to in summer.

S	T	R	O	H	S	P	I	T	T	R	S
L	E	W	O	T	I	C	O	R	P	U	P
A	E	S	T	A	E	H	A	O	N	☀	O
D	L	S	W	C	T	V	O	G	L	H	L
N	D	T	R	I	E	H	L	C	E	O	F
A	D	E	S	L	M	A	E	I	A	L	P
S	A	S	I	D	S	S	S	N	E	I	I
M	P	W	☀	S	I	H	U	C	N	D	L
H	C	A	E	B	E	T	H	I	O	A	F
U	R	S	A	L	A	D	K	P	T	Y	B
O	L	I	L	E	P	I	E	R	S	S	T
P	A	S	L	S	B	O	A	T	I	N	G

beach
bikini
boating
flip flops
heat
holidays
ice cream
lilo
paddle
picnic
pier
pool
salad
sandals
sea
shells
shorts
sunglasses
swimsuit
towel
travel

Hidden message:
Trips to the seaside with our best pals.

34

The Four Marys

THE Four Marys, Cotter, Simpson, Radleigh and Field, were best friends in the Third Form of St Elmo's school for Girls. One Saturday afternoon the girls visited the nearby town of Elmbury —

DID YOU BUY ANYTHING?

YES, THESE EARRINGS. THEY'RE REAL GOLD — BUT I GOT THEM FOR NEXT TO NOTHING. YOU NEED TALENT TO SPOT A BARGAIN.

TCH!

On Monday, Raddy visited the school library —

I WISH THEY'D GET SOME NEW BOOKS. I THINK I'VE READ THESE ALL AT LEAST TWICE!

THAT GIRL MUST BE NEW. AFTER I'VE CHOSEN A BOOK, I'LL GO ACROSS AND SAY HI!

But —

AAAH! WATCH WHERE YOU'RE GOING!

SORRY, MISS CREEF!

By the time Raddy had helped Miss Creef pick up the books, the girl had gone. But —

A SILVER LOCKET! THE NEW GIRL MUST HAVE DROPPED IT.

THERE MIGHT BE SOMETHING INSIDE TO SHOW ME WHO SHE IS.

36

But —

PHOTOGRAPHS OF TWO ST ELMO'S OLD GIRLS. MAYBE ONE OF THEM IS THE NEW GIRL'S MOTHER.

In the common room —

I FOUND THIS ON THE LIBRARY FLOOR. I THINK A NEW GIRL DROPPED IT.

YOU'D BETTER GIVE IT TO THE HEAD.

Just then —

I HOPE YOU DIDN'T PAY MONEY FOR THAT AWFUL LOCKET, RALEIGH. I CAN TELL FROM HERE THAT IT'S WORTHLESS JUNK.

OH, REALLY, MABEL? HOW COME IT'S STAMPED SILVER, THEN? AND FOR YOUR INFORMATION, I FOUND IT AND I'M TAKING IT TO MRS MITCHELL.

That night —

RING! RING!

THAT'S THE FIRE ALARM!

DON'T PANIC. LEAVE THE BUILDING IN AN ORDERLY MANNER.

WHERE'S THE FIRE?

I CAN'T SEE ANY FLAMES, COTTY.

HERE'S THE FIRE BRIGADE.

Half an hour later —

FALSE ALARM, GIRLS. THE FIREMEN HAVE DONE A THOROUGH CHECK OF THE BUILDING AND THERE'S NO SIGN OF A FIRE ANYWHERE.

UNLIKE FIFTY YEARS AGO.

WHAT DOES MISS CREEF MEAN?

TODAY IS THE FIFTIETH ANNIVERSARY OF A BAD FIRE AT ST ELMO'S. THAT NIGHT A GIRL DIED.

HOW AWFUL!

SPOOKY, I'D CALL IT.

EXACTLY FIFTY YEARS AFTER THE FIRST FIRE, WE HAVE A FALSE ALARM.

RADDY'S RIGHT, IT *IS* ODD. I'D LIKE TO KNOW MORE ABOUT THE OTHER FIRE.

LET'S DO SOME RESEARCH TOMORROW, SIMPY.

So next day, after tea —

HERE WE ARE. OLD NEWSPAPERS FROM FIFTY YEARS AGO.

LET'S TAKE THEM BACK TO OUR STUDY.

WHAT ON EARTH ARE YOU DOING WITH THESE MUSTY OLD FILES?

RESEARCH, MABEL. THERE'S SOMETHING WE WANT TO FIND OUT.

FANCY SPENDING THE EVENING WITH YOUR HEADS IN A DUSTY OLD BOOK! YOU FOUR ARE SO BORING! *WE'RE* GOING OUT.

AND I'M WEARING MY NEW EARRINGS. LOOK!

Soon —

ANY LUCK?

NOT SO FAR, FIELDY. BUT I . . . OH, WAIT A MINUTE!

HERE IT IS! THE GIRL WHO DIED WAS CALLED SOPHIE FERNIE. HER BEST FRIEND, ALICE PETRIE, TRIED TO SAVE HER, BUT COULDN'T. THERE ARE PICTURES OF THEM. LOOK.

FIRE AT ST. ELMO'S

IT'S THE TWO GIRLS IN THE LOCKET!

YOU'RE RIGHT, RADDY!

THIS IS SOPHIE FERNIE — THE GIRL WHO DIED.

...E AT ST. ELMO'S

SHE CAN'T HAVE BEEN THE NEW GIRL'S MOTHER, THEN. MAYBE IT WAS HER AUNT, OR SOMETHING. THERE'S CERTAINLY A FAMILY RESEMBLANCE.

Next day —

MRS MITCHELL HAS ASKED EVERYONE, BUT NO ONE HAS LOST A SILVER LOCKET. AS YOU FOUND IT, YOU CAN DECIDE WHAT TO DO WITH IT, RADLEIGH.

THANK YOU, MISS CREEF.

ONE OF THE PHOTOS IS ALICE PETRIE. MAYBE WE COULD TRACK HER DOWN AND GIVE IT TO HER?

GOOD IDEA, RADDY. LET'S ASK MRS MITCHELL IF SHE CAN FIND OUT WHERE ALICE CAME FROM.

40

And so —

MRS ALICE BOWMAN?

YES.

WE'RE FROM ST ELMO'S SCHOOL, AND WE HAVE SOMETHING FOR YOU.

MY LOCKET! WHERE DID YOU FIND IT?

IN THE SCHOOL LIBRARY.

THAT'S WHERE I LEFT IT — FIFTY YEARS AGO. I LOVED THAT LOCKET. WHEN A FIRE BROKE OUT IN THE SCHOOL, I STUPIDLY RUSHED INTO THE BUILDING TO LOOK FOR IT.

AND THAT'S WHEN YOU TRIED TO RESCUE SOPHIE?

NO! I WAS JUST A STUPID GIRL WHO RAN BACK INTO A FIRE. SOPHIE TRIED TO RESCUE ME — AND DIED IN THE PROCESS. SHE WAS THE HEROINE, NOT ME.

BUT THE PAPER SAID . . .

I KNOW. EVERYONE THOUGHT I'D TRIED TO RESCUE SOPHIE, AND I WASN'T BRAVE ENOUGH TO TELL THE TRUTH. I FELT AS IF I HAD CAUSED MY FRIEND'S DEATH, SO I KEPT MY GUILTY SECRET TO MYSELF — FOR FIFTY YEARS.

IT'S SUCH A RELIEF TO TELL SOMEONE THE TRUTH AT LAST. BUT HOW STRANGE THAT YOU SHOULD FIND THE LOCKET AFTER ALL THESE YEARS. WAS IT WELL HIDDEN?

NO. IT WAS LYING ON THE FLOOR. I THOUGHT A NEW GIRL HAD DROPPED IT. STRANGELY, SHE LOOKED A BIT LIKE THE PICTURE OF SOPHIE.

HOW DID YOU DISCOVER THAT THE PICTURES WERE OF SOPHIE AND ME?

OUR TEACHER TOLD US THAT IT WAS THE FIFTIETH ANNIVERSARY OF THE FIRE. WHEN WE LOOKED IT UP IN AN OLD NEWSPAPER, WE SAW YOUR PICTURES.

I SEE. BUT TELL ME, DO YOU KNOW THE NAME OF THE GIRL WHO DROPPED THE LOCKET?

NO. I'VE NEVER SEEN HER BEFORE — OR SINCE.

AND I DON'T THINK YOU'LL EVER SEE HER AGAIN. I — I CAN'T BE SURE, BUT I THINK IT MIGHT HAVE BEEN SOPHIE.

A GHOST?

I CAN'T THINK OF ANOTHER EXPLANATION. PERHAPS SHE WAS TRYING TO TELL ME SHE FORGIVES ME, BY RETURNING MY LOCKET.

I SUPPOSE THAT MUST BE IT. WOW!

A few weeks later —

IN MEMORY OF SOPHIE FERNIE

IT WAS A NICE IDEA OF MRS BOWMAN'S, TO DEDICATE A PLAQUE TO SOPHIE'S MEMORY.

YES. AND THE NEWSPAPER WILL RUN THE STORY — TELLING THE TRUTH AT LAST.

JUST AS WELL I DIDN'T THROW AWAY THE LOCKET LIKE MABEL SUGGESTED.

TALKING ABOUT JEWELLERY, HAVE YOU 'SPOTTED' ANYMORE BARGAINS RECENTLY, MABLE?

HA, HA, HA!

the end

HIDE 'N' SEEK!

Help Molly make her way through our mega maze to find her hidden mates.

START

FINISH

Solution on page 112

43

Weather Watch

We can't swear that all these weather signs are accurate — but they're a lot more fun than watching the forecast on TV.

If cows run for shelter in a shower, then the rain will be on for a long time. If, however, they stay in the open, then the rain won't last long.

Hang some seaweed up in the house. If it becomes damp it means rain is on its way.

A closed fir cone warns of cold, wet weather, while an open cone means the weather will be warm and dry.

If there are more swifts than swallows, then it is going to be a hot, dry summer.

A cow lying down is a sign of good weather.

Wood anemones only open their petals when there is a wind, and Michaelmas and Livingstone Daisies only open when it's sunny.

If fish swim near the surface of the water, it means rain. If they are sluggish, then watch out for thunder.

A lot of berries on a tree can be a sign of a bad winter approaching.

A swarm of ants travelling in an orderly line warns of storms, while scattered ants mean good weather.

Bees will not swarm while waiting a storm.

If dandelions bloom in early spring, then summer will be very short.

Curling leaves warn us that rain is approaching.

If your cat sits with her back to the fire, it means it's going to snow. If she washes behind her ears, then it's about to rain.

Seagulls sitting on roof tops means that a storm is on its way.

Spiders cannot spin webs in the wind, so it's said that if you see a spider spinning, there is probably wind on the way.

A lot of wasps collecting pollen means warm weather ahead.

If geese fly directly south, then a cold winter can be expected.

Toadstools springing up during warm weather is a sign that rain is on its way.

Sun before seven, brings rain by eleven!

A misty May means June will be warm.

And finally........if you go out and forget to take your umbrella, then it's almost SURE to rain!!!

PURR-

Does your cat take to her heels whenever you try to cuddle her? Do you sometimes think she just doesn't love you? Well, don't panic, because we're about to tell you how to turn your moody moggy into a purr-fect pet!

Try not to shout or have your TV or music blaring when your cat's around. Cats hate noise - so if she's unhappy, she'll just leave you and go off to find some place quiet where she can sleep.

Be gentle with her. Your cat is a small, delicate creature compared to you, and being too heavy-handed will scare her off.

Don't try to force cuddles on her. Remember how dreadful it was when your ancient relative tried to hug *you*? Well, your cat feels the same. When she *wants* you to cuddle her, she'll let you know.

When you feed her, tell her how good dinner will be. Sound enthusiastic, but speak softly. Stroke her a couple of times as she walks to her dish, then leave her to eat.

When you stroke or play with her, crouch down to the floor so you don't look so big and scary. Remember, you look like a *giant* to her.

Tickle her softly under her chin, around her cheeks and at the base of her tail. Her scent glands are here, and she'll love to leave her own special smell on your fingers.

FECT PET!

When your cat looks at you with half-closed eyes, or blinks at you slowly, she's saying, "I really love you!". And you can use her language to tell her that you love her back! Gaze at her with half-closed eyes and blink slowly three or four times. You'll make her **really** happy!

Spend time in the same room as her, even when you're not playing together. She'll love your quiet presence - even if you're only reading, doing homework, or watching TV.

Stroke her gently and often. Run your hand softly over her head, down her back and right along her tail to its very tip! Remember to be gentle! And if she doesn't want you to stroke her, leave her alone until she's ready.

Greet her like you would your best friend! Always say 'hello' and speak her name when you first meet her. Chatter to her in a soft voice whenever she's near.

Play with her often. If you buy her toys, always make sure they are proper cat toys. A fluffy ball on the end of a string is a really good toy, because you can play without touching her until she gets used to you.

Tickle behind her ears and tug them gently, or rub them lightly between your fingers. She can't easily reach them when she wants to scratch, so she'll love the feeling!

Finally, never shout at her - and **never** smack her! If she does something naughty, then hiss at her. That's the way her mum scolded her when she was a kitten! She'll remember that hiss, and soon learn to behave!

Friends For

Are you and your best mates set to be friends for life? We show you a way to find out. It may not be scientific – but it's certainly lots of fun to do!

Begin by writing your full name at the top, with the word **LIKES** underneath. Now put your friend's name below that and count how often the letters **L, I, K, E** and **S** appear in the two names.

Once you have done that, add the numbers together until you're left with only two numbers. This is your 'Friendship Rating'. It sounds a bit complicated, but our two examples show how easy it is to work out.

You can try this with all your friends if you like and, if you know middle names (and like adding up) it can be even more fun.

Once you've worked out all your Friendship Rating, why not think of all the lads you fancy and work out your 'Love Rating'. This works the very same way – except you substitute the word **LOVES** for **LIKES**

Have fun!

LAUREN DAVIS
L I K E S
SUZANNE KING

L = 1
I = 2
K = 1
E = 2
S = 2

1+2=3 2+1=3 1+2=3 2+2=4
3334

3+3=6 3+3=6 3+4=7
667

6+6=12 6+7=13
1213

1+2=3 2+1=3 1+3=4
334

3+3=6 3+4=7
67% Friendship Rating

TESS ANDREWS
L O V E S
BEN EDWARD

L = 0
O = 0
V = 0
E = 4
S = 3

0+0=0 0+0=0 0+4=4 4+3=7
0047

0+0=0 0+4=4 4+7=11
0411

0+4=4 4+1=5 1+1=2
452

4+5=9 5+2=7
97% Love Rating

Ever?

Now check what your ratings mean.

0% = 30%
FRIENDSHIP RATING
You obviously get on well enough, but you probably don't share your innermost secrets. You two may be friends, but you're not likely to be **best** friends.
LOVE RATING
You could be good friends, but it would be best to leave it at that because a romance isn't likely to work!

31% = 60%
FRIENDSHIP RATING
You don't **always** have to be in each other's company, but you've got lots in common and enjoy the same things, so you are likely to stay good mates for many years.
LOVE RATING
You may like him a lot, but this boy probably won't ever be more than a friend. Best look elsewhere for romance.

61% = 85%
FRIENDSHIP RATING
You two probably feel as if you've been friends for ever- and perhaps you have. You're sure to stay very close for years as you have so much in common.
LOVE RATING
This could be a match made in Heaven but, then again, it **could** be a disaster. Have fun finding out.

86% = 100%
FRIENDSHIP RATING
This is a friendship that will go on and on and on. You know each other inside out, and you'll probably still be best mates when you collect your pensions.
LOVE RATING
Wow! This guy is your Mr Perfect - according to the numbers, anyway. Hope he feels the same way about you!

WILD

Jane Landrie had a French pen-pal called Jolie. Jane wrote to Jolie in French and Jolie replied in English — which often gave Jane quite a laugh.

Just Like Jolie

I LOVE READING JOLIE'S LETTERS — ESPECIALLY WHEN SHE GETS MIXED UP WITH HER ENGLISH. IN THIS ONE SHE SAID THAT THE RAIN 'SOAKED HER WITH WET'!

OH, HERE'S A PHOTO OF JOLIE WITH HER BOYFRIEND, HENRI. MMM! HE LOOKS NICE.

'WE MET AT A CAFE BEFORE THE PARTY. YVETTE AND CLAUDE CAME, TOO.' JOLIE AND HER FRIENDS ALWAYS SEEM TO BE GOING OUT AND HAVING FUN.

SHE MUST THINK I'M A TOTAL BORE. THE MOST EXCITING THING I DO IS WINDOW-SHOP WITH ROZ ON SATURDAYS.

51

And —

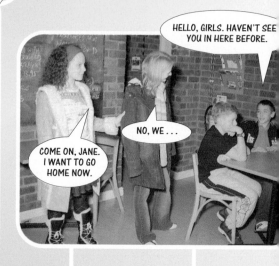

54

And —

55

top to toe!

What's your fashion fave?

Find out with our fabby flowchart.

START
Do you have lots of sparkly sandals?

N

Are you always rushing around?

You're a party person. True?

N

Do you collect groovy coloured nail varnishes?

It's sometimes difficult for you to make up your mind. True?

N

Are country walks a fave thing?

N

Do you own toe rings?

N

Are you sporty?

N

You rarely feel cold. True?

N

Is art a fave school subject?

N

Would you like to be a model?

N

Do you wear lots of jewellery?

N

You like walking barefoot. True?

N

You like walking barefoot. True?

N

You're a party princess who loves swishing about in skirts, showing off trendy toes in sparkly sandals! Cool colours and lots of bling are what you would choose, cos there's nothing you like better than standing out in a crowd.

Anything and everything, that's what you love! You like experimenting with fashion but, if you had to pick a fave item, it'd be tops, cos they can change the look of skirts or trousers from casual to disco diva in just a few seconds.

You're into casual gear and think skirts and heels are just plain silly. Life's too much fun to spend time deciding which shoes go with which skirt. You stick to boots and flat shoes with trousers for no-nonsense style!

IT HAPPENED TO ME....

WHEN Steve first spoke to me I was over the moon. After all, he was captain of the football and cricket teams, and sports champion, too. All the senior girls fancied him, so I couldn't believe my luck when he came over to me in the corridor and said how much he'd enjoyed watching me in the junior badminton tournament. Wow!

Who's got an admirer?" my friend, Lisa, giggled as Steve moved away. "Maybe he fancies you!"

I told her not to be stupid – but inside I was all mixed up. Steve couldn't **possibly** fancy a mousy little junior like me – could he?

★ ★ ★

The more I thought about it, the more I convinced myself that it might be true. After all, he **had** spoken to me. From then on I couldn't get Steve out of my mind. I was convinced that it was only a matter of time until he asked me out – but I didn't want to wait. I wanted it to happen **now!**

Picture posed by models.

I knew that Steve went running in the morning, so next day I dragged myself out of bed early and headed for the playing fields. Steve seemed a bit surprised to see me, but he smiled and said hi. My heart did a summersault!

The trouble was, although I was keen on some sports, running wasn't one of them and, after a week, I gave up trying very hard. I didn't give up going to the playing fields, though, but instead of running I just stood and watched Steve. I realise now how obvious I must have looked, but at the time I just didn't think. I wanted Steve to ask me out so I had to stay near him. It was as simple as that!

★ ★ ★

Then my world crumbled. I'd gone to the playing fields and was watching Steve go through his usual warm up routine when one of his mates looked over and started to laugh.

"Your shadow's here again," he shouted to Steve. " Why don't you tell her to push off back to nursery?"

I didn't catch what Steve said then, but the next thing I knew he was coming over. After all my efforts, he was at last going to speak to me again – but somehow I knew I wasn't going to like what he had to say.

★ ★ ★

And I was right. Steve was really nice about it, but he stated clearly that he didn't fancy me and didn't want to ask me out. He said he had been trying to encourage me by praising my badminton game – nothing more. He was sorry that I had a crush on him, but he just wasn't interested – and I was embarrassing him by hanging around all the time.

I didn't say anything as he turned away, but I felt so stupid I couldn't even cry. A crush – that was all it had been – a silly juvenile crush. In a way I was lucky because Steve could have been really cruel, but I vowed there and then that I'd **never** make such a fool of myself again.

Matchmaker!

ONE evening, while Cate and her friends were visiting their mate Lisa —

ONLY TWO MORE DAYS TILL YOUR SISTER'S WEDDING, LISA. ARE YOU EXCITED?

YOU BET, JESS. I'VE BEEN TRYING ON MY BRIDESMAID'S DRESS TWICE A DAY FOR THE LAST WEEK.

THIS IS IT. WHAT D'YOU THINK, GIRLS?

WOW! IT'S GORGEOUS. I LOVE THE COLOUR.

ME TOO. IT'LL REALLY SUIT YOU, LISA.

I WISH I COULD BE A BRIDESMAID AND WEAR A DRESS LIKE THAT. I REALLY ENVY YOU, LISA.

BUT YOU'VE GOT A BIG BROTHER AND SISTER, CATE. YOU'LL PROBABLY GET TO BE A BRIDESMAID BEFORE TOO LONG.

I DOUBT IT. STEVE LIVES UP NORTH AND BEV SPLIT WITH HER LAST BOYFRIEND SIX MONTHS AGO. I DON'T THINK SHE'S BEEN ON A PROPER DATE SINCE.

WELL, WHY NOT FIX HER UP WITH SOMEONE? BEV'S REALLY PRETTY.

MY BROTHERS *BOTH* FANCY HER LIKE MAD. MIND YOU, THEY'RE TWELVE AND THIRTEEN, SO I DON'T SUPPOSE SHE'D BE INTERESTED.

PROBABLY NOT, JESS. AT LEAST, NOT FOR ANOTHER TEN YEARS OR SO. ANYWAY, ENJOY SATURDAY, LISA, AND I'LL SEE YOU ALL SOON.

I KNOW I JOKE ABOUT IT, BUT I REALLY *WOULD* LIKE TO BE A BRIDESMAID SOON.

MAYBE I SHOULD DO WHAT SALLY SUGGESTED AND TRY TO FIND A BOYFRIEND FOR BEV. IT SHOULDN'T BE ALL THAT HARD, COS SHE *IS* REALLY PRETTY — AND FUN, TOO.

Next day —

HI, CATE. D'YOU WANT TWO TICKETS FOR THE BIG MOVIE ON SATURDAY? I BOUGHT THEM AS A SURPRISE FOR MY NEW GIRLFRIEND — BUT THEN *SHE* SURPRISED ME BY DUMPING ME.

POOR YOU, MIKE. BUT I'D LOVE THE TICKETS. THANKS.

OH, BUT WAIT A MINUTE! I-I'M ALREADY DOING SOMETHING ON SATURDAY. BEV'S FREE THOUGH. WHY — ER — WHY DON'T YOU ASK HER IF SHE'D LIKE TO GO WITH YOU?

PHEW! I THOUGHT OF THAT JUST IN TIME. MIKE'S THE PERFECT BOY NEXT DOOR.

COOL. I'LL PHONE BEV LATER. THANKS FOR SUGGESTING IT, CATE.

THIS COULD BE IT! I DON'T KNOW WHY I DIDN'T THINK OF MIKE AGES AGO.

And, on Saturday —

ENJOY YOURSELF, BEV.

I'M SURE I WILL. THE FILM'S SUPPOSED TO BE GREAT — AND MIKE AND I HAVE ALWAYS GOT ON REALLY WELL.

Later —

WELL, HOW WAS IT?

COOL. WE WENT FOR A PIZZA AFTER AND HAD A REAL LAUGH. IN FACT, WE'RE GOING OUT AGAIN NEXT WEEK.

BRILLIANT. BRIDESMAID'S DRESS, HERE I COME.

But —

SORRY, BEV, BUT MY EX-FIANCEE IS BACK IN TOWN AND WANTS US TO GET TOGETHER AGAIN. I'LL HAVE TO CANCEL OUR DATE.

THAT'S OKAY, MIKE. I UNDERSTAND.

THE RAT! I NEVER THOUGHT MIKE WOULD DUMP SOMEONE LIKE THAT. HUH!

DON'T PANIC, CATE. I KNEW HE WAS STILL KEEN ON JO — AND WE WERE ONLY GOIN' OUT AS MATES. I COULD NEVER THINK OF MIKE IN A ROMANTIC WAY.

OH, WELL, SO MUCH FOR THAT GREAT IDEA. BUT THERE MUST BE SOMEONE — MAYBE IN THE BANK WHERE BEV WORKS.

So —

I'LL PUT MY BIRTHDAY MONEY INTO MY ACCOUNT AND CHECK OUT THE TALENT WHILE I'M THERE.

RICK MASON

WOW! HE LOOKS NICE — JUST BEV'S TYPE. NOW, I WONDER HOW I CAN GET THEM TOGETHER OUTSIDE WORK.

QUEUE HERE

Cate's chance came that night —

OF COURSE YOU CAN HAVE SOME WORK FRIENDS ROUND, BEV. NO MORE THAN EIGHT, THOUGH, COS WE DON'T HAVE MUCH ROOM. AND CATE CAN INVITE A FRIEND FOR COMPANY, TOO.

THANKS, MUM. I'LL DRAW UP MY LIST TONIGHT.

THE LAST TIME I WAS IN THE BANK I NOTICED A REALLY GOOD-LOOKING GUY. RICK SOMEBODY. ARE YOU GOING TO INVITE HIM?

RICK MASON? NO. I DON'T THINK SO.

BUT HE LOOKS REALLY NICE. I HAVEN'T ASKED ANYONE YET, SO WHY DON'T YOU INVITE RICK IN PLACE OF MY FRIEND. I DON'T MIND.

WELL, WHATEVER YOU SAY, CATE. BUT I HOPE YOU DON'T HAVE PLANS TO CHAT HIM UP. HE'S MUCH TOO OLD FOR YOU.

BEV'S GOT IT ALL WRONG. *SHE'S* THE ONE WHO'S GOING TO END UP WITH RICK. THEY'LL MAKE A REALLY GOOD-LOOKING COUPLE.

But, on the night —

. . . SO I CALCULATED THAT THE BASIC RATE INTEREST WOULD BE . . .

OH, BOY! NO WONDER BEV WASN'T KEEN TO INVITE RICK. HE COULD BORE FOR BRITAIN.

GONE OFF RICK, HAVE YOU? HE MAY BE GOOD-LOOKING, BUT HE'S ALSO A TOTAL PAIN.

YOU CAN SAY THAT AGAIN.

ANOTHER ONE BITES THE DUST. BUT I *WILL* FIND THE BOY FOR BEV. HE'S GOTTA BE OUT THERE *SOMEWHERE.*

A few days later —

WOW! ISN'T HE GORGEOUS?

AT LAST! THIS CALLS FOR DRASTIC ACTION.

So —

AAGH! I'M SLIPPING!

CATE! HAVE YOU HURT YOURSELF?

IT'S MY ANKLE. I . . .

COOL! HE HEARD ME AND HE'S STOPPING.

And —

CAN I HELP? ARE YOU OKAY?

YEAH — I THINK SO. I JUST NEED TO SIT HERE FOR A MOMENT.

THAT SHOULD GIVE THEM TIME TO CHAT.

WHAT A BEAUTIFUL HORSE. WHAT'S HIS NAME?

SILVER. EM — YOU SEEM TO LIKE HORSES. HOW — HOW WOULD YOU LIKE TO COME HORSE RIDING WITH ME NEXT WEEKEND?

ER — NO THANKS. I-I'M BUSY. THANKS FOR YOUR HELP, BUT MY SISTER'S FINE NOW SO WE'D BETTER GO.

EH? I DON'T BELIEVE THIS.

WHY DID YOU TURN HIM DOWN? HE SEEMED REALLY NICE — AND GOOD-LOOKING, TOO.

YOU THINK SO? I DIDN'T FANCY HIM AT ALL!

BUT YOU *DID!* YOU SAID HE WAS *GORGEOUS!*

TCH! THAT WAS THE *HORSE* I WAS TALKING ABOUT. NOW COME ON, MUM'LL BE WONDERING WHERE WE ARE.

At home —

PREPARE YOURSELVES FOR A SURPRISE, GIRLS. WE'VE GOT VISITORS.

STEVE!

YEAH! AND I'D LIKE YOU TO MEET RACHEL — MY FIANCEE!

HI. YOU MUST BE BEV AND CATE! I'VE HEARD LOTS ABOUT YOU.

WE'RE PLANNING OUR WEDDING FOR THE SPRING, AND WE'D LIKE YOU *BOTH* TO BE BRIDESMAIDS.

COOL!

MY DREAM IS COMING TRUE AFTER ALL — ALTHOUGH NOT IN THE WAY I'D THOUGHT.

MY OLDER BROTHER HAS SEEN PHOTOGRAPHS OF YOU, BEV — AND HE CAN'T *WAIT* TO MEET YOU.

REALLY? WHAT'S HE LIKE?

AND WHO KNOWS! MAYBE THERE COULD BE *ANOTHER* WEDDING BEFORE TOO LONG.

THE END

SNAPPED!

Peepers poised for a page of perfect picture puzzles!

where in the world?
These pictures all show parts of very famous tourist attractions. Can you name them?

Groovy Girlies!
Can you name the three well known faces from the pictures? Clue: There's a singer, an actress and a TV presenter.

Soap Stuff!
All the people here appear, or have appeared, in TV soaps. For full points, name the soaps, the characters and their real names.

Spot the Difference!
These two pictures look the same but there are three small differences. Can you spot them?

Answers on page 112

ARIES
(March 21- April 20)
If there's something new to try out, then Miss Aries is the one to try it. This girlie is so full of energy she barely has time to sit down and relax. She should keep a tight grip on that temper of hers, though, before it lands her in *big* trouble. Lucky colours include yellow and gold and spring flowers - especially daffodils - are favoured by girls born under the sign of the ram.

- [ ] You're often in trouble at school.
- [ ] You've been called bossy.
- [ ] You can be stubborn at times.
- [ ] You like to be a leader.

TAURUS
(April 21- May 20)
Miss Taurus is into all things creative. She just loves to make things - especially friends. Old friends *and* new friends are very important to this chatty, reliable miss. She must beware of being clumsy, though. Just because her star sign is a bull, it doesn't mean she can behave like a bull in a china shop. Purple or pink are the best colours for Taurus girls.

- [ ] You call a spade a spade.
- [ ] You often break things.
- [ ] You like to get your own way.
- [ ] You're very determined.

GEMINI
(May 21- June 21)
Gemini girls do well at school because they love learning new things, especially languages and geography. They're popular with their classmates and are always coming up with new and novel ideas - although they often loose interest in things before very long. Gemini girls can also be a bit two-faced from time to time, so don't believe *everything* they say.

- [ ] You love to gossip.
- [ ] You tire of people quickly.
- [ ] You can be moody.
- [ ] You're easily bored.

There's a goody and a baddy inside each of us. To discover which is your ruling force, read your star sign, then tick any boxes that you think describe you. You can tick any number – even none – but be honest. To find the conclusions – and more signs – turn the page. Have fun!

CANCER
(June 22 - July 23)
Cancer is the sign of hoarding, so girls born at this time of year are likely to have bedrooms filled with 'treasures' of all kind. Cancer girlies hate to part with anything - and they certainly like to hold on to their friends. Though loyal mates, they can be a bit sulky if things don't go their way. Lucky colours are green and grey - and Monday is their *least* favourite day of the week.

- ☐ You've never told a fib.
- ☐ You remember everyone's birthday.
- ☐ You're a romantic at heart.
- ☐ You *always* try to be helpful.

LEO
(July 24 - August 23)
Leo girls are born leaders and will probably have a whole crowd of mates. Miss Leo loves explaining things and could make a good teacher. Leos are known to be brave - but like to show off at times, so can be a bit overpowering. Leo girls are also very, very determined and, once they reach a decision, it's almost impossible to make them change their mind.

- ☐ You've never said anything nasty to anyone.
- ☐ You'd like to do community work.
- ☐ Nothing scares you.
- ☐ You don't mind coming last.

VIRGO
(August 24 - September 23)
Virgo girls are kind and caring - if a little bit cautious - and usually have very good memories. They like to look their best at all times and make a good impression on people they meet. They make kind and thoughtful friends and will always be ready to listen and offer advice to those they care about. Mind you, they do like to gossip, so be careful what you say.

- ☐ You like housework.
- ☐ You've won prizes for neatness.
- ☐ You always pick up your clothes.
- ☐ You never criticise anyone.

LIBRA **(September 24 - October 23)**

Not surprisingly, girls born under this sign are well balanced are even-tempered. They really like to be liked - by everyone - and, as a result, they're very popular. They are also polite and are often first to volunteer if help is needed. Unfortunately, they tend to be a little bit lazy so, while they're quick to volunteer, they don't always actually *do* everything they promise to do.

SCORPIO

(October 24 - November 22)

Scorpio girls make loyal and caring friends - but don't cross them cos they can make powerful enemies, too. They also like to be leaders and may attempt to dominate those close to them. They are determined, quiet and thoughtful and tend to be very close to their families. Scorpio girls like reading and writing, so they often keep a diary with all their secrets inside.

- ☐ You're jealous of some friends.
- ☐ You'd cheat to pass an exam.
- ☐ You don't like sharing.
- ☐ You loose your temper easily.

SAGITTARIUS

(November 23 - December 22)

Honest, outgoing and optimistic are the words that best sum up Sagittarius girls, so this means that they are great fun to know. Unfortunately they can also be clumsy and thoughtless sometimes, so may occasionally offend people without meaning to. Sagittarius girls love the outdoor life, and will often choose to play or watch sport rather than go shopping.

- ☐ You always want your own way.
- ☐ You're sometimes very careless.
- ☐ You don't think before you speak.
- ☐ You've been called rude.

CAPRICORN

(December 23 - January 20)

If you are a Capricorn, then you're likely to be very well organised and trustworthy. Parents and teachers know that they can trust Miss Capricorn, so she will often find herself in charge - as class captain or school monitor, perhaps. On the downside, however, she can sometimes be a bit of a Scrooge with money. Capricorn girls often prefer counting cash to spending it.

- ☐ You put others' feelings before your own.
- ☐ You've never slept in.
- ☐ You do your homework before watching TV.
- ☐ You never fall out with friends.

- [ ] You usually lie in bed until called.
- [ ] You'd flirt with a mate's boyfriend.
- [ ] You don't like making decisions.
- [ ] You sulk to get what you want.

AQUARIUS
(January 21 - February 19)

Girls born under this sign are creative and full of good ideas. They love to have fun and are usually amongst the first to try new styles and fashions. A favourite day would be spent at the seaside or at a fair, riding the rollercoasters. Although Aquarius girls often give the impression of being rather vague and dreamy, they can be very stubborn when they want - so be warned.

- [ ] You share everything with friends.
- [ ] You'd rather give than receive.
- [ ] You've never played your music too loudly.
- [ ] You never say an angry word.

PISCES
(February 20 - March 20)

Daydreaming and reading are how Miss Pisces often chooses to spend the day. She loves hanging out with her mates, though, and is always willing to listen and help if any of them has a problem. Girls born under this sign tend to be imaginative and creative - but a bit impractical and lazy, too. Tuesdays and Saturdays are the best days for Pisces girls to shine!

- [ ] You'd never say no to a friend.
- [ ] You like dreams better than reality.
- [ ] You always get up with a smile on your face.
- [ ] You prefer celery to chocolate.

Now count how many boxes you ticked, and read the conclusions.

STAR FORCE! for
Aries, Taurus, Gemini, Libra, Scorpio and **Sagittarius**

If you ticked....

4. You're ruled by your Baddy - so beware. Try to be a bit less daring before it's too late.

3. You're a bit of a Baddy at heart - but you can behave sometimes - if you have to!

2. You're trying to be a Goody - and that's good. Just concentrate and you'll get there.

1. Your Goody is definitely your guide. You know how to behave *and* have fun.

0. There's such a thing as being too good, you know. A little bit of Baddy behaviour won't hurt *anyone!*

STAR FORCE! for
Cancer. Leo, Virgo, Capricorn, Aquarius and **Pisces**

If you ticked....

4. Oh, come on! You're not so much a Goody as a Goody two shoes. It's only natural to be a little bit of a Baddy. And it's fun!

3. You listen to your Goody almost always - but you have the odd slip. which *is* allowed!

2. You're a Goody and quite typical of your star sign. But be aware that your Baddy *is* around!

1. You'd like to be a Baddy, but you just can't pull it off. Why not be a Goody instead?

0. Either you fibbed, or you're a total Baddy. Which ever, you should give your Goody a chance.

Autumn

Find these words, hidden up, down, backwards, forwards or diagonally in our ace autumn wordsearch. Letters can be used more than once and, when you've finished, the unused letters will spell out something we should do on Hallowe'en.

T	L	O	Y	L	L	I	H	C	O	K	O
R	E	L	K	R	A	P	S	U	M	T	A
I	S	✿	P	U	M	P	K	I	N	P	F
C	S	G	O	M	P	R	S	L	P	O	E
K	T	U	U	W	A	T	F	L	L	G	Y
O	U	Y	K	B	I	D	E	E	N	H	T
R	N	F	R	O	N	S	G	A	W	O	S
T	T	A	A	N	I	T	R	V	C	S	E
R	S	W	D	F	H	O	A	E	✿	T	V
E	E	K	W	I	N	D	I	S	E	S	R
A	H	E	N	R	E	T	N	A	L	S	A
T	C	S	N	E	E	W	O	L	L	A	H

apples
bonfire
bugs
chestnuts
chilly
damp
dark
ghosts
Guy Fawkes
Hallowe'en
harvest
lamp
lantern
leaves
mist
orange
pumpkin
rain
sparkler
trick or treat
wind

Hidden message:
Look out for low flying witches!

TOOTS

LOOK AT THAT MODEL BEING PHOTOGRAPHED!

IT WOULD BE GREAT TO BE A MODEL.

"I'D WEAR FABBY CLOTHES AND JEWELS."

POSE IN EXOTIC PLACES.

"THE DESERT."

"THE JUNGLE."

"THE GREEK ISLANDS."

acting up!

Ever fancied attending a drama class? We asked some friends from the Activate Drama Group in Sunderland to let us into a few of their stage secrets.

How did you first become interested in drama?

Eleanor: I think I've always wanted to act. I was about five when I asked if I could go to classes.

Katie: My dancing teacher suggested I find out about classes, so my mum phoned up...

Sophie: ...and that was it!

Beth: I don't know exactly when my interest started. I've wanted to act since I was tiny.

Bethany: A friend's mum told my mum about the classes and I thought they sounded fun.

what kind of shows have you taken part in?

Emma: I've been on TV in *Byker Grove* and a drama called *Wire in the Blood*. I've also been in a Fire Brigade video called *Hoax*

Sophie: I've been in *Byker Grove* and have also taken part in a singing competition. I've done several shows at the Empire Theatre, too.

Eleanor: A Fire Brigade video and lots of choir work. I've also taken part in a Victorian show – which was fun.

Beth: I was in *102 Dalmatians* at the Odeon and have sung with my choir at the Royal Festival Hall. I've done lots of other things as well.

Do you want to make acting your career?

Sophie: Yes. Well, either that or a singer or dancer. I definitely want to be on the stage.

Bethany: I think so. I love acting because I can have fun and express myself.

Katie: I want to carry on acting. I'd quite like to be in adverts and things like that.

Emma: If I'm not an actress I'd like to be a waitress – maybe in my dad's restaurant.

Tell us a bit about your favourite performances.

Bethany: When I appeared in *Byker Grove* it was filmed on a boat called the Tuxedo Princess. I liked that.

Beth: My favourite of all was going to the Royal Festival Hall and singing with my choir. I love singing, and this was especially exciting.

Emma: I liked being in *Wire in the Blood* best. I was an extra in the background, and the wages were good.

Katie: I've loved most things I've done – especially the live shows. I've been in *Alice the Musical*, *Summertime Special*, *Christmas Capers* and *Santa in Space*. They were fun.

Sounds like you're all very busy. Do you have time for other hobbies?

Katie: I go to dancing and I also have singing lessons. I used to do gymnastics, but I gave it up.

Beth: I play the guitar, violin and keyboard – and I also like hockey, netball and swimming. I went to ballet and tennis lessons when I was younger.

Eleanor: I do gymnastics at school, and I really, really love writing stories.

Emma: I used to like tennis and horse riding, but now I'm into Irish Dancing and playing keyboard and flute – not all at the same time. I also like reading.

What would be your ideal role?

Sophie: I'd love to be in *EastEnders* as one of the Slater family. Or in *The Sound of Music*. That's my favourite film.

Eleanor: I'd like to be in any TV soap – but most of all I want to act in the theatre.

Emma: Anything comedy, because I love it. My favourite actors are Jim Carrey and Whoopi Goldberg.

Bethany: I'd choose *Mary Poppins*. Live theatre is great and it seems a really fun show.

And, finally, tell us something special about yourself.

Beth: I'd like to be one of the Moon family in *EastEnders*.

Eleanor: I love being really dramatic!

Emma: I want to be in *Coronation Street*.

Sophie: I'm addicted to TV talent shows.

Bethany: I used to do line dancing and won Dancer of the Year twice.

Katie: I regret not auditioning for the *Billy Elliot* musical.

Thanks, girls. We'll watch out for you on TV in the future.

WRITE ON!

What's it like to be a successful author while still at school? To find out, we spoke to Isabel Adomakoh Young. Along with her mother, Louisa Young, Isabel makes up the writing team of Zizou Corder - author of the acclaimed (and exciting!) Lionboy books.

Isabel and her mum, Louisa.

When did the idea of Lionboy first come about, and how?
The whole thing started with bedtime stories when I was about three, in 1996. Mum's written lots of other books since, though, so it hasn't taken all that time.

How much of the story is your idea and how much does your mum contribute?
We just chat about our ideas. We discuss what the people are going to do next, how they feel, whether there should be another shipwreck and should we bring the whale in yet and what we want in the circus - stuff like that. Then Mum writes it all down and I read it and tell her if it's any good.

The name Zizou is very unusual. How did you decide on it as a pen name?
Zizou is after our pet lizard, Zizu. Some people think it was after the footballer Zinedine Zidane, but that isn't true.

Is the character of Charlie Ashanti based on anyone you know and, if so, can you tell us who it is?
He's me and mum, mum and me - and all boys everywhere.

Have you ever really disagreed over any part of the book?
Only once. Mum wanted to kill somebody off and I didn't think it fitted in. Mum laughed - but I won. I won't tell you what it was because it'd spoil the story.

How did you feel when you saw your very first book in print?
Fizzy inside.

How did your friends react to you becoming an author?
They're not bothered - they're more interested in school football.

Have any of your friends read the books? What did they think?

We gave the people in my class a copy each and dedicated book one to them all. But then we studied it at school and we all ended up saying, "Oh, no! Not more Lionboy" because it went on for so long. Most of us had finished the book ages before.

Can you tell us a bit about it the third Lionboy book?

They go to Ghana and the Caribbean, and Maccomo comes back. There's a football team in it and a very grand finale in an evil headquarters. It'll probably be the last book - but you never know.

Have you plans for any further books?

Well, I'm moving up at school, so I may have to spend all my time doing homework. Also, Mum wants to do some grown-up stuff, but we're thinking about ideas all the time.

What's the best thing that's happened to you due to the success of Lionboy?

So many good things. Going to Thailand and hearing a gecko yelling by the pool!

Lionboy is set in the near future. If it were possible, would you rather live in the future or the past - and why?

The past, because we're going into the future anyway.

Apart from Lionboy, what is your all time favourite book.

That's hard because I love loads of books. This week it's probably anything by PG Wodehouse.

Do you want to be a full-time author when you're older? If not, what would you like to do?

I'd like to be an author, but not necessarily full-time. I want to do other things so I would have something to write about.

Which other country would you most like to visit?

Australia. I'd really like to see a kangaroo.

In the books, Charlie can speak 'cat'. If you had a choice, which animal language would you like to speak?

Lizard. I want to ask Zizu how he hurt his toe.

Finally, what advice would you give to other girls who want to be writers?

Read, write, read, write, pay attention - get your mum to do the typing.

Isobel's Faves

Actor -   Johnny Depp
Singer -   Eminem
TV prog -The Simpsons
Food -   Pizza
Film -   Some Like it Hot
Subject - English
Country -Thailand

Lionboy books are published by Puffin Books and are available from good book shops.

79

BELLA and Josie sat on the fence, gazing upwards at the black sky with its rolling dark clouds and scattered winking stars.

"Magic!" Bella sighed. "Don't you think it's cool, Josie?"

"No," Josie replied, hugging herself miserably. "It's just plain cold! Why wait till late October to go hunting werewolves?"

"Because it's the right thing to do at Hallowe'en. Besides, we've got Dad's tent, thermal sleeping bags and hot coffee — and if you're really cold, you can always go back to the house."

Bella and Josie lived next door to each other, their houses backing on to the moor. Bella had first heard the howling one night in the early spring. She'd listened to the eerie wail echoing across the moor and wondered what kind of animal could be making it. Then the newspaper reports started. Some people claimed to have seen the creature — a huge wolf type animal only ever sighted at the time of the full moon. A supernatural wolf. A werewolf!

Bella had spent hours sitting by her bedroom window when the moon was full, almost praying for the wolf to appear. But it never did. So eventually she'd persuaded Mum and Dad to let her camp out in the back garden and lie in wait for it. Mum and Dad didn't really believe the stories, so they had agreed — but only if Josie went with her.

Josie was really reluctant. She'd argued and complained for days — but finally she'd agreed to help her friend. So now she was sitting on the fence, shivering and miserable, while Bella grew more excited by the minute.

"It would be amazing to see it," Bella said to Josie cheerfully.

"I don't think it even exists," Josie snapped.

"Oh, yes it does!" Bella was adamant. "Werewolves are great ugly beasts, but I'm sure they exist. I've read lots about them and I'm sure it's a werewolf I heard on the moor."

"It's probably some poor, hungry dog." Josie sniffed.

"They retain a lot of their human characteristics," Bella ignored her friend's scathing remark. "Some people say they walk on their hind legs."

"Stupid!" Josie muttered under her breath.

Bella scanned the skies.

"The full moon's tucked just behind that cloud," she said. "When it passes by, the moon will light the whole moor. The howling will begin — just wait and see."

Josie fell silent. Her eyes, suddenly large and frightened, were fixed to the cloud. For the first time, Bella realised that her friend was actually afraid.

"Josie," she whispered, placing a hand on her friend's arm. "You're scared, aren't you? I didn't realise. I'm so sorry."

Josie never took her eyes from the cloudy sky.

"Yes," she said eventually. "I-I'm terrified!"

Bella shook her head.

"Gosh, Josie — you don't have to sit out here with me if you feel like that," she said kindly. "You can go into the tent — or even the house. So long as you're quiet, Mum and Dad won't know, and neither of us will get into trouble."

"I can't do that," Josie replied solemnly.

"Course you can," Bella laughed, hugging her comfortingly. "I'll be okay."

"You — you don't understand." Josie continued to stare at the sky, while large tears spilled slowly down her cheeks.

"Josie, what's wrong?" Bella gasped as

the full moon slid from behind the cloud, spilling bright silver light all around them.

✳ ✳ ✳

Slowly, as Bella watched, Josie's eyes began to change, sharpening from a soft brown to a vivid blue. Then her teeth began to grow, elongating into fangs that glinted in the light, and rich chestnut hair sprouted from her hands and face.

Bella gasped! Josie — her best friend Josie — was the werewolf.

As Bella stared in wonder, the beast threw back its head and howled its unbearably loud and mournful howl!

Bella looked long and hard at the creature she had dreamed of glimpsing. She was so shocked, she couldn't breathe. But it wasn't because of the terrifying changes she had seen. And it wasn't because her best friend was a werewolf. It was something else.

"Oh, Josie," she eventually gasped. "You — you're not ugly — you're beautiful."

And, as Bella smiled, the huge wolf stepped forward and gently stroked her hand.

The End

81

Feel The Heat!

Are you too cool? Or just cool enough?

START
Friends often ask for your advice. True?

Find out with our fun flowchart!

N → Can you keep a secret?

Y → Do you like playing sports?

Can you keep a secret?
- **N** → Are you good at telling jokes?
- **Y** → Will you happily try new things?

Do you like playing sports?
- **N** → Will you happily try new things?
- **Y** → You want to wear the latest fashions. True?

Are you good at telling jokes?
- **Y** → Do you love a good gossip?
- **N** → Would you like to be a designer?

Will you happily try new things?
- **N** → Would you like to be a designer?
- **Y** → A best friend's better than a group of mates - true?

You want to wear the latest fashions. True?
- **Y** → A best friend's better than a group of mates - true?
- **N** → Do you always tell the truth?

Do you love a good gossip?
- **Y** → Can you laugh if you make a mistake?

Would you like to be a designer?
- **N** → Can you laugh if you make a mistake?

A best friend's better than a group of mates - true?
- **N** → Do you always tell the truth?
- **N** → You love being the centre of attention. True?

Do you always tell the truth?
- **Y** → Art is your fave school subject - true?

Can you laugh if you make a mistake?
- **Y** / **N** → Sorry, but you're not very cool!

You love being the centre of attention. True?
- **Y** / **N** → Yes, you are cool!

Art is your fave school subject - true?
- **Y** / **N** → You're very cool, with a quiet, serious side.

Sorry, but you're not very cool! You're a kind, warm person who has loads of mates. Friends feel they can talk to you about anything and are certain you'll try your best to help them with any kind of problem.

Yes, you are cool! Everyone knows that you're game for a laugh and ready to try anything new. You'll be in charge of arranging most things for your gang of mates - and you'll love it! And you know what? So will they!

You're very cool, with a quiet, serious side. You're always up-to-date on the latest things to see, do and wear, so friends will often ask for your advice. You're happy enough in a group but also enjoy your own company.

Living Legends!

Are you a playful pixie, loyal leprechaun or bashful brownie?
Try our fun quiz and find out!

1. The school fete wants old toys for the bring and buy stall. What would you do?
a) Happily hand over all your teddies and dolls, cos you're too old for them now.
b) Refuse to part with anything. You love your toys too much.
c) Set to work and make some soft toys to hand in.

2. Your best friend's new baby sister has just arrived home. How would you react?
c) Go round to see her once everyone has settled in.
a) Rush over with lots of presents for the baby. You can't wait to see her.
b) Promise to visit the baby soon - once she's outgrown the smelly, noisy stage.

3. The school is organising a big fund-raising event and asks for volunteers. Which of these would you be most likely to do?
b) Nothing. You don't have any free time and there will be lots of other helpers.
a) Come up with lots of ideas - for other people to do.
c) Gather all your mates together and offer to help out in any way you can.

4. On a camping adventure trip, what would be your favourite activity?
b) Horse riding. You'd love it!
c) Cooking and toasting marshmallows round the campfire.
a) Paragliding or gliding in a plane.

5. You find a trick spider in the room. Which of these would you do?
a) Put it on the sofa where it'll give Mum a scare.
c) Throw it in the bin in case it gives someone a fright.
b) Leave it on the floor and see if anyone else notices.

A new girl
arts at school.
ow are you
ost likely to
eact?
 Offer to show
her round and
introduce her to all
the teachers and
pupils.
) Tell her that all
new girls have to
report to the Head
for 'a long stand'.
b) Make her
welcome - but
hope she doesn't
steal your mates.

7. At the school disco,
where are you most likely
to be found?
b) In the middle of
the dance floor, giving it all
you've got.
a) Sitting chatting
with your mates and eyeing
up the boys.
) Dancing on the
edge of the floor, or in a
corner.

. You need to
nd a fancy
ress outfit in a
urry. What
ould you do?
c) Start making
things from
cardboard and pipe
cleaners.
a) Take money
from your bank and
hire one.
b) Throw a sheet
over your head and
go as a ghost.

Now check out your results.

Mostly a Pixie

You're a mischievous pixie who loves playing tricks and making jokes. You love babies and are at your happiest when in a crowd of mates. Pixie people are usually quite dainty and are sometimes said to bring good luck wherever they go - making them very popular. But even pixies have their faults - like talking too much. Your mouth doesn't always have to be open, you know.

Mostly b Leprechaun

Like leprechauns, you love music, dancing and having fun. You don't suffer fools gladly, but when you make a friend you will be loyal for life. Legends say that if you catch a leprechaun all your wishes will come true - and that's probably how your friends feel about having you as a mate. On the minus side, you can be very possessive - and a little mean, too.

Mostly c Brownie

Brownies like to keep themselves to themselves, but are very helpful to others. Although they seem shy, they are good at standing up for their rights and are unlikely to be bullied. They make good, caring friends - although they may not always show their feelings in public. Brownie's tend to be dark, with large eyes and gentle smiles - but they can be a little bit sly, so watch out!

THE SECRET!

WHEN her widowed mother died, Sarah Gray spent two weeks in a home before going to live with her cousin Polly and her family.

I HOPE YOU'LL BE VERY HAPPY WITH US, SARAH.

AND IF THERE'S ANYTHING UPSETTING YOU, PLEASE DON'T HESITATE TO SAY.

POOR SARAH. HER MUM'S BEEN ILL FOR YEARS, BUT IT MUST STILL BE AWFUL TO LOSE HER.

WE THOUGHT YOU'D BE HAPPIEST WITH A ROOM OF YOUR OWN. POLLY WILL HELP YOU UNPACK.

JUST LEAVE ME ALONE. I CAN MANAGE.

HMM! SARAH'S HARDLY THE FRIENDLY TYPE. STILL, WE HAVE TO MAKE HER FEEL WELCOME.

OH! RIGHT! I-I'LL GIVE YOU A CALL WHEN TEA'S READY.

87

89

93

DID YOU KNOW....?

Justin Timberlake

Justin Timberlake was born in Memphis

Christina Aguilera has two sisters, Rachel and Stephanie, and two brothers, Michael and Casey.

Ashley is two minutes older than **Mary-Kate**.

Beyonce is allergic to perfume.

When she was six years old, **Nicola**, **Girls Aloud**, dressed as a bunch of grapes for a fancy dress party.

Pink thinks she looks like a frog.

Dick and Dom once left their bungalow and gatecrashed 'Blue Peter'.

McFly's name comes from a character in the 'Back to the Future' films - Marty McFly.

James, ex-Busted, lists 'Back to the Future' as one of his favourite films. (Wonder if that means he's a **McFly** fan!)

Rachel Stevens loves driving to **Kylie**'s 'Can't Get You Out Of My Head'.

Gareth Gates is allergic to oranges.

Geri Halliwell loves porridge.

Fearne Cotton's fave school subjects were painting and drawing.

Harry, McFly once made a ten hour journey for a date.

Ant, will young and Dec

Emma watson and Daniel Radcliff

oadsa wowsome facts about celebs ast, present — and possibly future — for ou to wonder at!

Britney has always wanted to be a Bond Girl. Her fave food is pizza.

Kelly Osbourne sucks her thumb.

Tom, McFly once appeared in a background shot of 'EastEnders' and the whole band featured in an episode of 'Casualty'.

Anastacia is well into Doritos.

Daniel (Harry Potter) Radcliffe would like to play the drums.

Mark Owen's earliest memory is of stroking a bee which was sitting on his arm.

Hermione Granger may be a real swotty clogs, but **Emma Watson**, the actress who plays her, is a super sporty gal.

Hilary Duff's bedroom has a circus theme!

Keisha from the **Sugababes** can turn her ears inside out!

Ant and Dec had their first hit, 'Let's Get Ready To Rhumble' in 1994. At that time they were known as PJ and Duncan.

Nicky from **Westlife** and **Rachel Stevens** are both scared of lifts.

Will Young was once given Odor Eaters for Christmas.

Pink would love to play the violin.

Kevin from **V** used to like keeping ferrets.

Dick and Dom used to share a flat together.

Kelly Osbourne's fave word is 'awful'.

Justin Timberlake uses vanilla flavoured lip balm

Blue were originally called Lotus.

Nadine, Girls Aloud, loves fake tan.

Avril Lavigne sometimes uses her phone to record her songs.

Turn over for more celeb fact fun!

Hilary Duff

Fearne Cotton

McFly

CELEB CRED CHECK!

You've read the feature - now do the quiz to discover just how much you remember. No cheating, though!

1. What did Nicola from Girls Aloud once dress as for a fancy dress party?
a. A carrot
b. A bunch of grapes
c. A banana

2. From which films did McFly take their name?
a. Star Wars
b. Men in Black
c. Back to the Future

3. Who loves driving to Kylie's 'Can't Get You Out Of My Head'?
a. Rachel Stevens
b. Cher
c. Madonna

4. What has Britney always wanted to be?
a. An air hostess
b. A Bond Girl
c. A make up artist

5. Who is 'super sporty'?
a. Emma Watson
b. Janet Jackson
c. Kelly Osbourne

6. Who has sisters called Rachel and Stephanie?
a. Gery Halliwell
b. Britney Spears
c. Christina Aguilera

7. Hilary Duff's bedroom has which of the following themes?
a. Seaside
b. Circus
c. Rainforest

8. Who once gatecrashed Blue Peter?
a. Ant and Dec
b. Dick and Dom
c. Richard and Judy

9. Nicky from Westlife and Rachel Stevens share a fear of what?
a. Spiders
b. Lifts
c. Birds

10. Who once received Odor Eaters for Christmas?
a. Robbie Williams
b. Prince William
c. Will Young

11. Which instument would Pink love to play?
a. Piano
b. Violin
c. Saxophone

12. Who sang 'Let's Get Ready To Rhumble'?
a. McFly
b. PJ and Duncan
c. Justin Timberlake

13. Whose favourite word is 'awful'?
a. Gareth Gates
b. Britney
c. Kelly Osbourne

14. What flavour of lip balm does Justin Timberlake prefer?
a. Ginger
b. Vanilla
c. Chocolate

15. Who would love to play the drums?
a. Rachel Stevens
b. Mary-Kate and Ashley
c. Daniel Radcliffe

Now turn back to check your answers and discover your Celeb Cred rating!

12 - 15 You're either brilliant, or you cheated.
8 - 11 Your Celeb Cred's about right. Well done.
4 - 7 Mmm! Are you sure you read the feature before you did the quiz?
0 - 3 Oh, boy! Do you even know what a celeb is?

The Comp

NOT LONG NOW! ONLY A FEW MORE DAYS OF TORTURE TO GO!

HEY, MAYBE THE BUS WON'T GET THROUGH THE SNOW, AND THEN WE'LL GET TO GO HOME!

NO SUCH LUCK, ROZ! HERE IT COMES!

It was nearly the end of the Christmas term at Redvale Comp. One morning —

HOPE THE SNOW LASTS. IT ALWAYS FEELS MORE LIKE CHRISTMAS WHEN IT'S SNOWING.

Suddenly —

OHH! THE BUS IS SKIDDING!

LAURA!

AAAGH!

SORRY. WE HIT A PATCH OF BLACK ICE. HOW'S THE GIRL?

SHE'S UNCONSCIOUS. WE'D BETTER GET AN AMBULANCE!

NURSE JUNE SAID YOU'VE GOT CON-CONFUSION OR SOMETHING. DO YOU WANT TO PLAY A GAME? I'VE GOT LOTS.

NOW, ALICE, DON'T PESTER LAURA!

I DON'T MIND. I'D LIKE TO PLAY, ALICE.

And so —

I'VE WON!

YOU'RE FAR TOO GOOD FOR ME!

YOUR GRAN'S HERE TO SEE YOU, ALICE. OFF YOU GO!

ARE YOU BETTER, DEAR? THE DOCTOR SAYS YOU CAN REMEMBER YOUR ACCIDENT NOW.

YES, I'M FINE. WHAT HAPPENED TO ALICE, NURSE? CAN YOU TELL ME?

IT'S VERY SAD. SHE WAS PARALYSED IN A CAR CRASH THAT KILLED BOTH HER PARENTS. BUT SHE'LL BE GOING HOME TO HER GRAN SOON.

That evening —

CAN WE SEE LAURA BRADY, PLEASE? WE'RE HER BEST FRIENDS.

OF COURSE. LAURA'S MUCH BETTER — WE'LL BE LETTING HER OUT TOMORROW.

OOPS!

HA, HA! SORRY!

ALICE! WATCH IT, YOU LITTLE MONSTER! YOU'LL GET A SPEEDING FINE IF YOU'RE NOT CAREFUL.

I SEE YOU'VE MET OUR ALICE! ISN'T SHE AMAZING?

SHE'S LIKE A RACING DRIVER IN THAT CHAIR!

SHE WON'T HAVE IT FOR MUCH LONGER, THOUGH.

WHAT DO YOU MEAN?

WELL, WHEN SHE GOES SHE'LL HAVE TO LEAVE OUR SPECIAL CHAIR BEHIND AND USE AN ORDINARY ONE.

THERE'S NO WAY HER GRAN CAN AFFORD TO BUY A CHAIR LIKE THAT.

OH, WHAT A SHAME!

COULDN'T WE DO SOMETHING TO HELP?

HOW ABOUT OUR SCHOOL CHARITY FUND-RAISING? EVERY YEAR IT GOES TO A DIFFERENT CAUSE, RIGHT? WELL, IF YOU THREE GO TO GRIM GERTIE . . .

And —

. . . SO WE WONDERED IF THIS YEAR'S MONEY COULD GO TOWARDS BUYING A SPECIAL WHEELCHAIR FOR ALICE.

THAT SOUNDS LIKE AN EXCELLENT IDEA, BECKY. I'LL MAKE ENQUIRIES AS TO THE COST.

Soon —

I'M SORRY, GIRLS, BUT WE DON'T HAVE QUITE ENOUGH. WE WOULD NEED ANOTHER FIVE HUNDRED POUNDS!

WE COULD RAISE IT!

THERE'S NEARLY A WEEK OF SCHOOL LEFT! COULD WE DO SOME EXTRA FUND-RAISING, MISS GRIMSTYLE?

103

But, on the night —

IT'S ALL WORKING! 'MY MUM SAYS' MARGARET *LOOKS* A BIT ODD, BUT SHE REALLY DOES HAVE A LOVELY VOICE.

THE DANCERS ARE GREAT! I DON'T KNOW WHAT BECKY WAS WORRYING ABOUT!

At the end —

VERY WELL DONE, EVERYBODY — AND SPECIAL CONGRATULATIONS TO THE DIRECTOR, BECKY SINDEN. I AM PLEASED TO TELL YOU, WE HAVE RAISED THE GRAND SUM OF . . .

. . . FIVE HUNDRED AND TWO POUNDS, FORTY-FIVE PENCE!

WE'VE DONE IT!

YE-ESSS!

Soon —

FOR ME? FOR KEEPS?

HOW CAN WE EVER THANK YOU?

I THINK WE CAN INVITE THEM ALL TO OUR CHRISTMAS PARTY, DON'T YOU?

And so —

THANK YOU SO MUCH, MISS GRIMSTYLE.

SOMETHING GOOD CAME OF MY BUS ACCIDENT, AFTER ALL. IT REALLY *IS* A MERRY CHRISTMAS!

the end

WILD

Merry CHRISTMAS!

START

Pull a cracker. If you win, take an extra throw. If you lose, miss a turn.

Bah, humbug! Miss a turn!

2

Miss a turn — or go outside and sing two verses of Jingle Bells.

4

5

10

9

7

Make a paper hat. If it falls off, go back four.

It's Christmas!!! Go forward three.

12

13

14

Hang Christmas baubles from your ears — or go back two spaces.

16

It's Christmas!!! Go forward two.

18

19

Have fun with this cool Christmas game. Any number can play and the youngest goes first. Throw a dice and move from space to space, following any instructions you may land on. The first one to throw the exact amount and reach home is the winner. Simple.

Eat a mince pie or chocolate deccie. Miss a turn if you don't.

38

Abolish Christmas. GO BACK TO START.

27

There's a hole in your stocking. Go back four.

Choose a Christmas song and sing it — or miss a throw.

36

FINISH

25

Offer to help Santa deliver gifts. Go forward four.

Bah, humbug! Miss two turns!

35

23

Secret Santa awards you an extra throw.

30

It's Christmas!!! Go forward four.

21

31

Move to the space occupied by the person on your right.

33

As a Christmas gift give the person on your left your turn next time round!

word POWER!

No numbers, no mazes, no tricks - just good old word power puzzles. Enjoy!

All Square

Solve the clues, then fit the words into the word squares. The only problem is, we haven't told you which clue is for which square but, to help, we've filled in a few letters. *Have fun.*

Across:
1. Black bird / ripped
2. Finished / thick string
3. Close to / the end of a prayer
4. Finishes / to curve

Down:
1. A particular sound / a type of shellfish
2. Capital of Italy / cooker
3. What we do with books / not closed
4. Make one's way / makes mistakes

Pyramids

Solve the clues to build the word pyramids.

Hat * Scenic view * Gets aw

Tear * Rubbish * Patterned

Animal Antics

Change **CAT** to **DOG**, **RAM** to **COW**, **DEER** to **STAG** and **PONY** to **GOAT** in as few moves as possible.

CAT	RAM	DEER	PONY
- - -	- - -	- - - -	- - - -
- - -	- - -	- - - -	- - - -
DOG	COW	- - - -	- - - -
		STAG	- - - -
			GOAT

Criss Cross

Eyes down for our quick crossword.

Clues

Across:

1. Pleasure.
7. Not off.
8. Pan for cooking.
10. Used for writing.
11. Travel on a ship.
12. Exists.
15. Hot drink.
17. Opposite of outside.
20. Cold _ _ ice.
21. Sharp pain.
22. Scottish girl.
24. Supernatural.
25. To compete.
26. Expression of surprise.
27. Sounds like the second letter.
28. Where to find peas.
29. Grain.
30. Twisted cord or string.

Down:

1. Galloping animal.
2. Indefinite article.
3. Remove skin.
4. Not nasty.
5. Broken in two.
6. Therefore.
9. _ _ and fro.
10. Outdoor meal.
13. The beach.
14. Baby pig.
16. Fools.
17. Irritating.
18. Check rudely.
19. The twelfth letter.
21. Fly high.
23. A river.
28. A Greek letter.

A E I O U

The vowels have been removed from the words below. Each word features only one vowel so, when there are two spaces, it is the same vowel in each space. All five vowels **must** be used - so what are the words? Tip: Leave the first word until last.

a) H _ T   b) T _ _   c) _ L _ S   d) _ C _ NG   e) C _ _ K

And finally

Fit the five colours into the grid in the correct order and the letters in the shaded squares will spell out the name of another colour.

BLUE
ORANGE
PINK
PURPLE
YELLOW

Answers on page 112

BARKING

You love your dog – of course you do – but are you sometimes driven crazy trying to understand what he's 'saying' to you? Read on and everything will be revealed!

When your dog rolls over to show his tummy, he's saying, "You're the boss, and I'll do anything you say!". This is especially true if he shows his tummy to another dog. Of course, with people he's sometimes just saying, "Tickle me – I love it!".

What if your dog puts his tail between his legs? Well, he's saying he's a bit worried about something. If he tucks his tail right under his bottom, he's saying, "I'm scared!".

Sometimes your dog may circle round and round before going to sleep. He's making sure he lies with his head pointing north. He knows that sleeping aligned with the Earth's magnetic field will help him stay especially healthy.

Your dog will also want to sniff other dogs – and even people. Usually he will sniff around their noses, but he may want to sniff other parts! Don't worry – it might not be polite in human circles, but this is a normal way for your dog to introduce himself.

If your dog grabs your hand or wrist, or chews your fingers or clothes, he's saying, "I like you and I'm really pleased to be with you!".

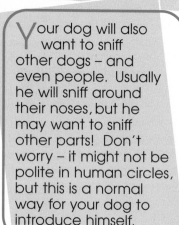

Most dogs want to be part of a group or pack, so house pets think of the family as their pack. That's why your dog is so delighted when he goes for a family walk – he's showing off his pack!

MAD!

If your dog struts towards another dog with his legs stiff, he's saying, "I'm top dog here! Do you agree, or do you want a fight?". Even worse, he may start to circle the dog and growl. If the other dog doesn't give in, it's best to move away quickly.

Sometimes your dog may eat grass. If he does this, it usually means he has a sore tummy. He knows the grass will make him sick, and he'll probably feel a whole lot better after.

If your dog suddenly starts tearing around a park or field with his bottom close to the ground, he's saying, "I really love and trust you, and don't mind acting really crazy while I'm with you!".

If your dog stares hard at someone, he's challenging them. If he avoids looking at them, it means he doesn't want any trouble and if his eyes are partially closed, he's probably nervous and wants you to stay away.

And a wagging tail doesn't just mean he's happy. It can mean he doesn't like you, or he's nervous. It can even be threatening. Look at how he's standing. Is the fur raised on his back and neck? Is he showing a lot of teeth? If a dog is showing a lot of teeth, he's definitely *not* smiling, and you should watch out!

Remember, good friends listen as well as talk. Listen to your dog, and you'll be the best friend he's got!

Your dog will try to lick people and other dogs to taste their scent. This answers questions your dog wants to ask, like, "Are you afraid? Are you angry? Are you happy?".

Puzzle Answers

HIDE 'N' SEEK!
Page 43

WORD POWER! Pages 108/109

All Square

```
TORE
OVER
NEAR
ENDS
```

```
CROW
ROPE
AMEN
BEND
```

Pyramids

```
    A
   CAP
  SCAPE
 ESCAPES
```

```
    I
   RIP
  TRIPE
 STRIPES
```

SNAPPED!
Page 65

Where in the World?
The Tower of London
The Trevi Fountain, Rome
The Great Wall of China

Animal Antics

CAT	RAM	DEER	PONY
COT	RAW	DEAR	POSY
DOT	ROW	SEAR	COSY
DOG	COW	STAR	COST
		STAG	COAT
			GOAT

Groovy Girlies!
Fearne Cotton **Avril Lavigne** **Keira Knightly**

Soap Stuff!

Jennifer Ellison	Brookside	Emily Shadwick
Tina O'Brien	Coronation St	Sarah Louise Platt
Ryan Thomas	Coronation St	Jason Grimshaw
Joe Swash	EastEnders	Mickey Miller

Criss Cross

```
 H A P P I N E S S
 O N   E   I     P O T
 R   P E N C I L   O
 S A I L   E     I S
 E   C   P     T E A
   I N S I D E     A S
 S T I N G     L A S S
 O C C U L T   V I E
 A H   B E   P O D S
 R Y E   T W I N E
```

Spot the Difference!

AEIOU a) Hut b) Tee c) Alas d) Icing e) Cook

And Finally orange, **purple**, **blue**, yellow, **pink**. The hidden colour is **green**.

112

The Four Marys

THE Four Marys, Cotter, Field, Radleigh and Simpson, were in Elmbury doing their Christmas shopping. St Elmo's snobs, Mabel and Veronica, were also in town —

"OUT OF THE WAY, YOU KIDS!"

"YEAH, CLEAR OFF! MABEL AND I HAVE IMPORTANT CHRISTMAS SHOPPING TO DO."

A few minutes later —

"THE SERVICE HERE IS AWFUL, ISN'T IT, VERONICA?"

"HOW TRUE, MABEL! THIS ASSISTANT'S HOPELESS."

Meanwhile, in another part of Elmbury —

"THAT'S US FINISHED OUR CHRISTMAS SHOPPING NOW. WE'VE DONE REALLY WELL."

"IT'S GREAT THAT WE'RE ALL GOING TO SPEND CHRISTMAS AT RADLEIGH HALL, RADDY."

"YEAH! AND I'M LOOKING FORWARD TO YOU ALL BEING THERE, COTTY."

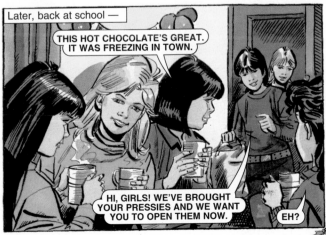

Later, back at school —

"THIS HOT CHOCOLATE'S GREAT. IT WAS FREEZING IN TOWN."

"HI, GIRLS! WE'VE BROUGHT YOUR PRESSIES AND WE WANT YOU TO OPEN THEM NOW."

"EH?"

THESE ARE LOVELY. THANKS VERY MUCH.

A few minutes later —

I DON'T GET IT. WHAT ARE MABEL AND VERONICA UP TO?

MAYBE THEY'RE JUST TRYING TO BE NICE, SIMPY. IT'S NEARLY CHRISTMAS, AFTER ALL.

WHAT'S GOING ON HERE? THE SNOBS HAVE NEVER BOUGHT US PRESENTS BEFORE.

YES, THANKS.

Meanwhile —

WELL, I THINK THAT WORKED, VERONICA. I DIDN'T LIKE HAVING TO DO IT, BUT WE FOOLED THEM!

OH, YEAH? THEY'VE NEVER SHOWN US ANY CHRISTMAS SPIRIT BEFORE, SO WHY NOW?

BEATS ME, BUT LET'S JUST GIVE THEM THE BENEFIT OF THE DOUBT THIS TIME.

YEAH. THEY'VE NO IDEA THAT WE KNOW THEIR SECRET.

THANKS TO US 'ACCIDENTALLY' GOING INTO THEIR STUDY THE OTHER DAY AND SEEING THAT LETTER FROM RADDY'S PARENTS, TELLING HER ABOUT PRINCESS SHEERA'S VISIT.

SHE'S KEEPING IT VERY QUIET. IF I HAD A PRINCESS COMING FOR CHRISTMAS, I'D TELL EVERYONE!

THE OTHER MARYS ARE INVITED THOUGH. IT MAKES ME SICK. IMAGINE THEM SPENDING TIME WITH A PRINCESS!

DON'T WORRY, MABEL. WE'LL GET INVITED, TOO. I'LL SEE TO THAT!

114

WELL, THERE WERE TWO OTHER GIRLS IN THERE LAST WEEK. WE SAW THEM.

TCH! ON THE FLOOR BELOW, NO DOUBT. THOSE FIRST YEARS SHOULDN'T EVEN *BE* HERE!

Later —

ISN'T SHE BEAUTIFUL, VERONICA?

YEAH — JUST LOOK AT THAT GORGEOUS OUTFIT!

I'D GIVE ANYTHING FOR THE CHANCE TO MEET PRINCESS SHEERA OF MONDAVIA, WOULDN'T YOU, VERONICA?

SO *THAT'S* WHAT IT'S ALL ABOUT! NOW WE KNOW WHY THEY'RE BEING NICE.

And —

THAT FITS WITH WHAT THOSE FIRST YEARS SAID. IT MUST HAVE BEEN MABEL AND VERONICA IN OUR STUDY. AND THEY'VE OBVIOUSLY READ RADDY'S LETTER ABOUT PRINCESS SHEERA COMING TO RADLEIGH HALL THIS CHRISTMAS. WHAT A CHEEK!

THAT'S WHY THEY WERE PRACTISING CURTSIES. WHAT A LAUGH! WELL, I THINK WE SHOULD MAKE USE OF THEIR 'FRIENDLINESS', DON'T YOU?

So —

WE THOUGHT, AS IT'S CHRISTMAS, WE COULD HELP ORGANISE THE LOCAL CHILDREN'S PARTY. ARE YOU TWO WILLING TO HELP?

OF COURSE — WE'RE WILLING TO DO *ANYTHING!* AREN'T WE, VERONICA?

Soon —

LOOK AT MABEL AND VERONICA! THEY'RE *HATING* THIS!

YEAH, BUT THEY'RE PRETENDING TO BE HAPPY — AND WE ALL KNOW WHY!

116

Next day —

ARE YOU SURE YOU'RE HAPPY TO LOOK OUT ALL THE CHRISTMAS DECORATIONS. IT'S A BIT DUSTY UP HERE.

OH, WE DON'T MIND, WE JUST WANT TO HELP.

So —

GOSH, I'VE NEVER SEEN THIS HALL LOOK SO CLEAN. WE CAN ALL HELP WITH THE DECORATING TOMORROW.

WE WORK WELL AS A TEAM. IT'S A PITY WE CAN'T ALL BE TOGETHER AT RADLEIGH HALL FOR CHRISTMAS.

OH, BUT WE COULD BE — I MEAN, WE'RE NOT DOING ANYTHING VERY SPECIAL.

WE'D LOVE TO COME TO RADLEIGH HALL — ER — JUST SO WE COULD ALL BE TOGETHER, OF COURSE.

I'VE PUT THEM OUT OF THEIR MISERY AND INVITED THEM. I'M SURE THEY'RE GOING TO LOVE MEETING PRINCESS SHEERA.

And, on Christmas Eve —

IT'S SO LOVELY TO BE HERE IN YOUR BEAUTIFUL HOME, MARY.

IS — IS EVERYONE ELSE HERE?

YES — INCLUDING PRINCESS SHEERA. I BET YOU DIDN'T KNOW SHE'D BE HERE!

OH, I — OF COURSE I DIDN'T.

SHE'S ABSOLUTELY BEAUTIFUL. I'VE BEEN HELPING HER SETTLE IN.

HUH! I'M SURE PRINCESS SHEERA WILL SOON REALISE WE'RE MORE THE SORT OF PEOPLE SHE OUGHT TO MEET!

118

WILD

Winter

All these words are hidden in our chillin' winter wordsearch. They can read up, down, backwards, forwards and diagonally, and letters can be used more than once. When you have found all the words, the remaining letters will spell out a festive message.

M	C	R	A	C	K	E	R	S	E	R	R
E	Y	C	H	S	E	V	O	L	G	R	I
S	T	B	T	N	A	M	W	O	N	S	M
M	❄	A	O	A	E	S	F	R	O	S	T
I	R	A	K	X	M	N	N	A	D	E	T
S	A	M	T	S	I	R	H	C	H	G	U
T	E	A	P	B	M	N	P	O	Y	D	R
L	Y	N	O	F	O	E	G	E	L	E	K
E	W	R	W	R	T	Y	E	D	❄	L	E
T	E	A	S	A	N	T	A	I	A	S	Y
O	N	R	H	C	A	T	O	L	A	Y	L
E	C	I	L	S	P	R	E	S	E	N	T

boxing day
carols
Christmas
~~crackers~~
~~frost~~
gloves
hat
holly
ice
mistletoe
new year
pantomime
present
robin
santa
scarf
skate
sledge
slide
snowman
turkey

Hidden message:

Merry Christmas and Happy New Year to all.

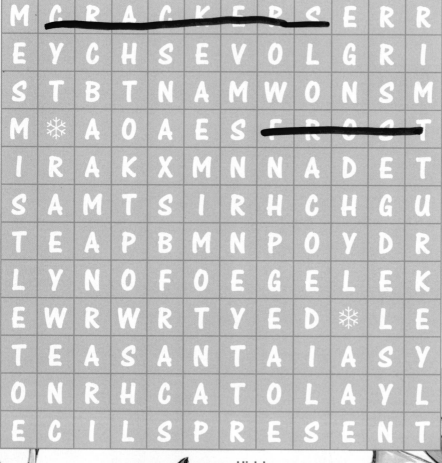

120

122

123

Julie explained —

HUH! I NEVER THOUGHT *MEL* WOULD BE IMPRESSED BY MONEY.

BUT CHEER UP, JULIE. YOUR PARTY'S GONNA BE GREAT — AND IT'LL BE MEL WHO MISSES OUT!

I KNOW THEY'RE RIGHT. BUT THE PARTY JUST WON'T BE THE SAME WITHOUT MEL. AND — AND IT'S AWFUL TO THINK THAT I MAY HAVE LOST MY BEST FRIEND.

On Friday —

THIS IS BRILLIANT. THE BEST PARTY I'VE BEEN TO IN MONTHS.

IT'S THE *ONLY* PARTY YOU'VE BEEN TO IN MONTHS, ANGIE.

WELL IT'S *STILL* GREAT. NOW, WHERE'S DAVE HILL GOT TO?

SHE'S CRAZY — BUT I SUPPOSE THAT'S WHY WE LIKE HER.

THAT'S YOUR PHONE, JULIE. IT'S MEL.

MEL! WHAT ON EARTH DOES SHE WANT?

HI, JULES, IT'S ME. I KNOW IT'S A BIT LATE, BUT WOULD — WOULD IT BE OKAY IF I CAME OVER NOW?

SUIT YOURSELF. BUT I KNOW WHERE YOU'VE BEEN. I KNOW YOU CHOSE TO MEET UP WITH LISA GRANGER RATHER THAN BE WITH ME.

THE END

A month by month guide

July

The month for coming off on holiday. If your school breaks up at the beginning of the month, then you've got lots of time to organise days out with your mates or trips to the seaside. If you don't come off until later, then enjoy all the end of term fun. And, now that Wimbledon's over, you can take to the tennis courts. Fresh air and exercise will keep you looking good – and you **could** turn out to be the next big British star.

August

It doesn't matter whether you're going away or staying at home, you should make August your holiday month. Have a competition with your mates to see who can send the funniest/ prettiest/most boring postcard. You have to send at least one – even if yo go no further than the corner shop. And the prize? A stick of rock, of cours

September

School is well and truly back this month – but don't despair, cos September can be a great month for picnics and barbecues. Have a back-to-school barbie for all your mates – and invite mums and dads, too, so they can do the cooking. September's also a good time to give yourself a totally new look for the new season.